"Please stay. Let my son live with you and Hetta," Andrew asked.

"But it's *you* he wants."

"I'll visit as often as I can."

"That's not enough."

He met her eyes. "Then I'll move back in."

"Let us understand each other," she said in a voice that was steadier than she felt. "You wish me to be your housekeeper and childminder."

"Very well. Housekeeper and childminder."

"All right," she said very quietly. "I'll do it."

It would be hard. He saw her as a convenience. But at least now she would not have to leave him—yet.

Lucy Gordon cut her writing teeth on magazine journalism, interviewing many of the world's most interesting men, including Warren Beatty, Richard Chamberlain, Roger Moore, Sir Alec Guinness and Sir John Gielgud. She also camped out with lions in Africa, and had many other unusual experiences which have often provided the background for her books. She is married to a Venetian, whom she met while on holiday in Venice. They got engaged within two days.

Two of her books have won the Romance Writers of America RITA® Award, *Song of the Lorelei* in 1990, and *His Brother's Child* in 1998 in the Best Traditional Romance category.

You can visit her Web site at www.lucy-gordon.com

Books by Lucy Gordon

HARLEQUIN ROMANCE®
3780—THE ITALIAN'S BABY
3799—RINALDO'S INHERITED BRIDE
3807—GINO'S ARRANGED BRIDE

HIS PRETEND WIFE

Lucy Gordon

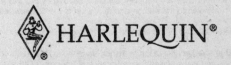

HARLEQUIN®

TORONTO • NEW YORK • LONDON
AMSTERDAM • PARIS • SYDNEY • HAMBURG
STOCKHOLM • ATHENS • TOKYO • MILAN • MADRID
PRAGUE • WARSAW • BUDAPEST • AUCKLAND

ISBN 0-373-03816-X

HIS PRETEND WIFE

First North American Publication 2004.

Copyright © 2002 by Lucy Gordon.

www.eHarlequin.com

Printed in U.S.A.

PROLOGUE

HE WOULD never have known her.

He would have known her anywhere.

Andrew caught only the briefest glimpse of the woman, at the far end of the hospital corridor, but it was enough to revive memory, as soft as a bird's wing fluttering past his face.

She looked nothing like Ellie, who'd been young and luscious as a ripe peach. This was a thin, pale woman, who looked as though life had thrown everything at her, and left her exhausted. Yet there was a hint of Ellie in the resolute set of her head and the angle of her jaw. The bird's wing fluttered again, and vanished.

He couldn't afford sentimentality. He was a busy man, second in command of the Heart Unit of Burdell Hospital. Ultimately he could only be satisfied with heading the team, but there was no shame in being second when the chief was Elmer Rylance, a man of international eminence. Soon he would retire and Andrew would step into his shoes.

He'd fast-tracked, giving everything to his work, allowing no distractions, as a broken marriage could testify. He was young for his position, although he didn't look it. His tall figure was still lean, his features handsome, and there was no grey in his dark hair, but his face had a gaunt look from too many hours spent in work, and not enough spent in living. And there was something about his eyes that spoke of an inner withering.

He had only time for a glimpse of the woman, enough to show that she was with a child, a little girl of about seven, on whom her eyes were fixed with an anguished possessiveness with which he was all too familiar. In this place he'd seen a thousand mothers look at their children like that. And usually his skill sent the two of them home happy. But not always. He turned swiftly into his office.

His secretary was there before him, the list of appointments ready waiting on his desk, along with the necessary files, the coffee being made, exactly as he liked it. She was the best. He only employed the best, just as he only bought the best.

The first patient on his list was seventeen, the age that Ellie had been. There the likeness ended. His patient was weary with illness. Ellie had been an earth nymph, vibrant with life, laughing her way through the world with the confidence of someone who knew she was blessed by the gods, and laughter would last for ever.

'Mr Blake?' Miss Hasting was eyeing him with concern.

He shook himself out of his reverie. 'I'm sorry, did you speak?'

'I asked if you'd seen the test results. They're just here…'

He grunted, annoyed with himself for the moment of inattention. That was a weakness, and he always concealed weakness. Miss Hasting was too well disciplined to notice. She was a perfectly functioning machine. Like himself.

Ellie's beauty had been wild and overflowing, making him think of wine and sun, freedom and splendour: all the good things of life that had been his for such a brief time.

He switched the thought off as easily as he would have switched off the light behind an X-ray. He had a heavy day ahead.

Besides, it hadn't been her.

'Time for me to start on my ward rounds,' he told Miss Hasting briefly. 'Make a call to...' For five minutes he gave brisk instructions.

When he went out into the corridor again the woman was gone.

He was glad of that.

CHAPTER ONE

SHE would have known him anywhere, any time. Down the length of the corridor. Down the length of the years.

Years that had changed her from a flighty, blinkered young girl who'd thought the world danced to her merry tune, to a bitter, grieving woman who knew that the world was something you had to fight. And you could never, ever really win.

She'd been partly prepared, seeing his name on the hospital literature. Andrew Blake was a common name, and it might not have been him, but she knew at once that it was. Just two words on the page, yet they had brought before her the rangy young man, too tense, too thoughtful, a challenge to a girl who'd known any man could have been hers if she'd only snapped her fingers. So she'd snapped. And he'd been hers. And they'd both paid a bitter price.

She'd planned a glamorous, if ill-defined, career for herself. She would earn a fortune and live in a mansion. The reality was 'Comfy 'n' Cosy', a shabby boarding house in a down-at-heel part of London. The paint peeled, the smell of cabbage clung, and the only thing that was 'comfy' was the kindness of her landlady, Mrs Daisy Hentage.

Daisy was peering through the torn lace curtains when the cab drew up, and Elinor helped her daughter onto the pavement. Once Hetta would have protested, 'I can manage, Mummy!' And there would have been a mother/daughter tussle, which would have made Elinor feel desperate. But now Hetta no longer argued, just wearily did as she was told. And that was a thousand times worse.

Daisy had the front door open in readiness as they slowly climbed the stone steps. 'The kettle's on,' she said. 'Come into my room.' She was middle-aged, widowed, and built like a cushion.

She scraped a living from the boarding house, which sheltered, besides Elinor and her daughter, a young married couple, several assorted students, and 'that Mr Jenson' with whom she waged constant war about his smoking in bed.

When the house was full Daisy had only one small room left for herself. But if her room was small her heart was large, and she'd taken Elinor and her little girl right into it. She cared for Hetta while Elinor was out working as a freelance beautician, and there was nobody else the distraught mother would have trusted with her precious child.

After the strain of her journey Hetta was ready to doze off on the sofa. When they were sure she was safely asleep they slipped into the kitchen and Daisy said quietly, 'Did you see the great man in person, or did you get fobbed off?'

'Elmer Rylance saw me. They say he always sees people himself when it's bad news.'

'It's much too soon to talk like that.'

'Hetta's heart is damaged and she needs a new one. But it has to be an exact match, and small enough for a child.' Elinor covered her eyes with her hand and spoke huskily. 'If we don't find one before—'

'You will, you will.' Daisy put her arms around the

younger woman's thin body and held her as she wept. 'There's still time.'

'That's what he said, but he's said it so often. He was kind and he tried to be upbeat, but the bottom line is there's no guarantee. It needs a miracle, and I don't believe in miracles.'

'Well, I do,' Daisy said firmly. 'I just know that a miracle is going to happen for you.'

Elinor gave a shaky laugh. 'Have you been reading the tarot cards again, Daisy?'

Daisy's life was divided between the cards, the runes and the stars. She blindly believed everything she read, until it was proved wrong, after which she believed something else. She said it kept her cheerful.

'Yes, I have,' she said now, 'and they say everything's going to be all right. You can scoff, but you'd better believe me. Good luck's coming, and it's going to take you by surprise.'

'Nothing takes me by surprise any more,' Elinor said, drying her eyes. 'Except—'

'What?'

'Oh, it's just that I thought I saw a ghost today.'

'What kind of a ghost?' Daisy said eagerly.

'Nothing, I'm getting as fanciful as you are. How about another cuppa?'

'It's not fair for you to be facing this alone,' Daisy said, starting to pour.

'I'm not alone while I've got you.'

'I meant a feller. Someone who's there for you. Like Hetta's dad.'

'The less said about Tom Landers, the better. He was a disaster. I should never have married him. And before him was my first husband, who was also a disaster. And before him…' Elinor's voice faded.

'Was that one a disaster too?'

'No, *I* was. He loved me. He wanted to marry me, but I threw him over. I didn't mean to be cruel, but I was. And I broke his heart.'

'You couldn't help it if you didn't love him.'

'But I did love him,' Elinor said softly. 'I loved him more than I've ever loved anyone in my whole life, except Hetta. But I didn't realise it then. Not for years. By then it was too late.' Anguish racked her. 'Oh, Daisy, I had the best any woman could have. And I threw it all away.'

There was more than one kind of ghost. Sometimes it was the other person, teasing you with memories of what might have been. But sometimes it was your own younger self, dancing ahead of you through the shadows, asking reproachfully how she'd turned into you.

To Ellie Foster, sixteen going on seventeen, life had been heaven: an impoverished kind of heaven, since there had never been money to spare in her home or those of her friends, and there had been a lot of 'making do'. But there had been the freedom of having left school. Her mother had tried to persuade her to stay on, perhaps even go to college, but Ellie had regarded that idea with horror. Who needed boring lessons when they could work in the cosmetics department of a big store? She'd seized on the job, and had had a wage packet and a kind of independence.

Best of all, she'd been gorgeous. She'd known it without conceit because boys had never stopped following her, trying to snatch a kiss, or just looking at her like gormless puppies. That had been the most fun of all.

She'd been tall, nearly five-foot eight, with a slender, curved figure and endless legs. She'd worn her naturally blonde hair long and luxuriant, letting it flow over her shoulders. To her other blessings had been added a pair of deep blue eyes and a full mouth that had been able to suddenly beam out a brilliant smile. She'd had only to give a man that smile...

What appalled Elinor, as she looked back over the years, was her own ignorance in those days. With just a few puny weapons she'd thought she could have the universe at her feet. Who had there been to tell her otherwise? Certainly not the love-struck lads who'd followed her about, practically in a convoy.

They'd formed a little gang, Pete and Clive and Johnny, Johnny's sister Grace, and another girl who'd tagged along because Ellie had always been the centre of the action, and being part of her entourage meant status. She'd been a natural leader, that had gone without saying. And she wouldn't be stuck long in Markton, the featureless provincial town where she'd been born. She could be anything she wanted. A model perhaps, or a television presenter, or someone who was famous for being famous. Whatever. The cosmetics counter had only been temporary. The city lights had beckoned, and, after that, the world.

Her seventeenth birthday had been looming, and as Grace had had a birthday in the same week both sets of parents had got together and held the party at Grace's home, which had been bigger. Ellie had a new dress for the occasion. It looked like shimmering gold and was both too sophisticated and too revealing, as her scandalised mother had protested.

'Mum, it's a party,' Ellie said in a voice that settled the matter. 'This is how people dress at parties.'

'It's much too low,' her mother said flatly. 'And too short.'

'Well, if you've got it, flaunt it. I've got it.'

'And you're certainly flaunting it. In my day only a certain kind of woman dressed like that.'

Ellie collapsed laughing. The things mothers said, honestly! But she gave Mrs Foster a hug and asked kindly, 'When you were my age, didn't you ever flaunt it?'

'I didn't have it to flaunt, dear. If I'd had—well, maybe I'd have gone a bit mad, too. But then I'd have lost your father. He didn't like girls who "displayed everything in the shop window".'

Ellie crowed with delight. 'You mean he was as much of a stick-in-the-mud then as he is now?'

'Don't be unkind about your father. He's a very nice, kind man.'

'How can you say that when he wanted to hold you back, stop you having fun?'

'He didn't. He just wanted me to have my fun with him. So did I. We loved each other. You'll find out one day. You'll meet the right man, and you won't want any fun that doesn't include him.'

'OK, OK,' Ellie said, not believing a word of it, but feeling good-natured. 'I just don't want to meet the right man until I've done a bit of living.'

Oh, the irony of having uttered those words, on that evening of all evenings! But she only came to see it later.

'Let's get to this party,' Mrs Foster said indulgently. 'You're only young once.'

Ellie kissed her, delighted, though not surprised, to have got her own way again.

The party overflowed with guests, with noise and merriment. The parents hung around for the first hour, then bowed to the unmistakable hints that were being thrown at them, and departed to the peace of the pub, leaving the young people alone. Someone turned up the music. Someone else produced a bottle of strong cider. Ellie waved it away, preferring to stick to light wine. Life was more enjoyable with a clear head.

The music changed, became smoochy. In the centre of the room couples danced, not touching, because that wasn't 'cool', but writhing in each other's general direction. She beckoned to Pete and he joined her, his eyes fixed longingly on her gyrating form. She was smooth and graceful, moving as though the music were part of her.

At first she barely glimpsed the stranger in the doorway, but then a turn brought her back to face him, and she saw that he was taller than everyone else in the room, and looked a little older. He wore a shirt and jeans, which were conservative compared to the funky teenage clothes around him.

What struck her most of all was his expression, the lips quirked in a wry smile, like a man showing indulgence to children. Obviously he thought a teenage rave beneath his dignity, and that made her very annoyed.

It wouldn't have mattered if he clearly belonged to another generation. Older people were expected to be stuffy. But he was in his twenties, too young for that slightly lofty look, she thought.

Nor would she have minded if he'd been unattractive. But for a man with those mobile, sensual lips to

be above the crowd was a deadly insult. His lean features made matters worse, being slightly irregular in
a way that was intriguing. His eyes were a crime too,
dark, lustrous and expressive. They should be watching her, filled with admiration, instead of flickering
over everyone with a hint of amusement.

'Who's that?' she yelled to her partner above the
music.

'That's Johnny's brother, Andrew,' he yelled back,
glancing at the door. 'He's a doctor. We don't see
much of him here.'

Johnny was weaving his way over to his brother.
Ellie couldn't hear them through the music, but she
could follow their greeting, the way Johnny indicated
for Andrew to join the party, and Andrew's grimace
as he mouthed, 'You've gotta be kidding.'

She followed Johnny's reply, 'Aw, c'mon.'

And Andrew's dismissive, 'Thanks, but I don't
play with children.'

Children. He might as well have shouted the word.
And her response, as she later realised, was childish.
She put an extra sensuousness into her writhing,
which made the boys shout appreciation and the girls
glare. She'd show him who was a child.

But when she looked up he'd gone.

She found him in the kitchen half an hour later,
eating bread and cheese and drinking a cup of tea.
She'd switched tactics now. Charm would be better.

'What are you hiding out here for?' she asked,
smiling. 'It's a party. You should be having fun.'

'I'm sorry, what did you say?' He raised his head
from the book he'd been reading. His eyes were un-
focused, as though part of him was still buried in the
pages, and he didn't seem to have noticed her smile.

'It's a party. Come and have fun. Don't be boring out here.'

'Better than being boring in there,' he said, indicating the noise with his head.

'Who says you're boring?'

He shrugged. 'I would be to them.' His tone suggested that he wasn't breaking his heart over this.

'So live a little.'

'By "live" you mean drink too much and make a fool of myself? No, thanks. I did that in my first year at Uni, and who needs to repeat an experience?'

He was dividing his attention between Ellie and his book, making no secret of the fact that she couldn't go fast enough for him.

'You mean *we're* boring, don't you?' she demanded, nettled.

He shrugged. 'If the cap fits.' Then he looked up from the book, giving her his whole attention. 'I'm sorry, that was rude of me.'

'Yes, it was,' noticing that his smile was gentle and charming.

'What's the party about?'

'It's my birthday—and Grace's.'

'How old are you?'

'Nineteen.' He laid down the book and regarded her, his head on one side. 'All right, not quite nineteen,' she admitted.

He looked her up and down in a way that made her think he was getting the point at last, but when he spoke it was only to say, 'Not quite eighteen, either.'

'I'm seventeen today,' she admitted.

'Don't sound so disappointed. Seventeen is a lot of fun.'

'How would you know? I'll bet you were never seventeen.'

He laughed at that. 'I was, but it's lost in the mists of time.'

When he grinned he was very attractive, she decided. 'Yes, I can see you're very old. You must be at least twenty-one.'

'Twenty-six, actually. Ancient.'

'No way. I like older men.' She was perching on the edge of the table now, crossing her legs so that their silky perfection was on display.

'Really?' he said, meeting her eyes.

'Really,' she said in a husky voice, full of meaning.

He picked up the book. 'Go back to your party, little girl. And be careful what you drink.'

'I think that's up to me,' she said defiantly.

'Sure. Enjoy the hangover.'

She glared but he wasn't looking. There was nothing to do but flounce out of the kitchen, slamming the door behind her. So she did it.

She found Johnny drinking cider.

'Your brother's insufferable,' she snapped.

'I could have told you that. Dull as ditch water. I don't know what made him arrive home tonight of all nights. He's supposed to be studying for his exams.'

'I thought he was already a doctor.'

'He is. He qualified last summer. This is a different lot of exams. He's always studying for something. Forget him and enjoy yourself. Here.' He poured some cider into a glass for her and she drank it in one gulp. Johnny immediately refilled her glass and she drained it again.

Out of sight she clutched the edge of the table. Not for the world would she have done anything so uncool as reveal how it was affecting her. She took a deep breath against the swimming of her head, and held out her glass.

'Fill it up,' she commanded with bravado.

He did so, and from somewhere there was an admiring cheer. Encouraged, she seized the big plastic bottle and drained it.

When she took the floor again she found that something had happened to her. Her limbs were mysteriously light, she danced as if floating on air and her whole body seemed infused with sensuality. Partners came and went. She didn't know who she was dancing with from one moment to the next, but she knew that none of them was the one she wanted.

'Hey,' she said, suddenly aware that there was a pair of unfamiliar arms about her, and she was being urged towards the door. 'Who are you?'

'You know me,' somebody whispered against her mouth. It was a man, but she couldn't think who he was. 'And you fancy me, don't you?'

'Do I?'

''Course you do. You're up for it, I can tell. Hey, what do you think you're doing?' The last words were addressed to someone who'd appeared out of nowhere and was determinedly freeing Ellie from the man's arms. 'Clear off.'

'No, *you* clear off,' came Andrew's voice.

'Now, look here—'

'Get lost before I do something very painful to you,' Andrew said, speaking almost casually.

'He will too,' Ellie remarked to nobody in particular. 'He's a doctor, so he'd know how.' The whole thing suddenly seemed terribly funny and she collapsed in giggles. Strong arms held her up, but now they were Andrew's arms.

'Thank you, kind sir,' she said with dignity, 'for coming to my rescue like a knight in shining armour.'

'What the devil have you been drinking?' Andrew demanded, not sounding at all like a gallant knight.

'Dunno,' she replied truthfully. 'It's a party.'

'So because it's a party you have to pour filthy rubbish down your throat and make a fool of yourself?' he said scathingly.

'Who are you calling a fool?'

'You, because you act like one.'

'Push off,' she said belligerently. The scene wasn't going at all as it should. 'I can take care of myself.'

'Oh, yeah!' he said, not even trying to be polite. 'I've seen children who can take better care of themselves than you. Come on.'

He'd taken a firm hold of her, but not in the way that other young men tried to. More like a man clearing out the rubbish. Ellie found herself being propelled firmly to the door.

'What d'you think you're doing?' she demanded.

'Taking you home.'

'I don't want to go home.' She tried to struggle but he had his hand firmly around her waist. 'Let *go*!'

'Don't waste your energy,' he advised her kindly. 'I'm a lot stronger than you.'

'Help!' she yelled. *'Abduction! Kidnap! Help!'*

That made them sit up, she was glad to see. Heads turned. Pete appeared, blocking their path.

'Where are you taking my girl?' he said belligerently.

'Who said I was your girl?' she demanded, briefly diverted. 'I never—'

'Shut up, the pair of you,' Andrew said without heat. 'She's not your girl because you don't know how to look after her. And you—' he tightened his grip on Ellie as she tried to make a bolt for it '—you aren't old enough to be anybody's girl. You're just a daft little kid who puts on fancy clothes and her mother's make-up and thinks she's grown up. Now, let's get out of here.'

'I don't want to get out of here.'

'Did I ask what you wanted?' he enquired indifferently.

'You'll be sorry you did this.'

'Not half as sorry as you'll be if I don't.'

She redoubled her efforts to escape, but he simply lifted her off the floor and left her kicking helplessly as he pushed Pete aside and strode on. Her head was swimming from the cider and her limbs were growing heavy, but through the gathering mist of tipsiness she could see her friends sniggering at her plight.

But then—relief! Johnny appeared, also trying to block their path.

'Put her down,' he said. 'She's my girl.'

'Another one?' Andrew said ironically. 'Listen, Johnny, I'll deal with you later. Just now I'm taking Ellie home where she'll be safe. What's her address, by the way?'

'Don't tell him,' she raged.

But Johnny had seen his elder brother's face and decided on discretion. He gave Andrew the information with a meekness that made Ellie disgusted with him. Before she could tell him so she found she was being carried out of the room. As the door swung to she was sure she could hear a burst of laughter, and it increased her rage.

Outside the house stood the most disgusting old van she'd ever seen. She couldn't believe he actually meant her to travel in that, but he was opening the door and shovelling her into the passenger seat. Shovelling was the only word for it. She immediately tried to break out and he slammed the door shut again.

'We can do this the easy way, or the hard way,' he said through the half-open window. 'The easy way is for you to sit here quietly. The hard way is for me to chuck you in the back, lock the rear doors and keep you there until we reach the other end.'

'You wouldn't dare.'

He grinned. 'Even you're not stupid enough to believe that.'

'Whaddaya mean? *Even* me?'

'Work it out.'

As he went around to the driver's seat she sat in sullen silence, partly because she knew he meant what he said, and partly because it was becoming hard to move. She leant her head against the back of the seat, just for a moment.

CHAPTER TWO

'ARE you all right, darling?' Mrs Foster's face came into focus.

'Mum? What—?'

Somehow the van had turned into her own bed in her own room. Her head was throbbing and her mother was smiling at her anxiously.

'How did I—? Oh, goodness!'

She bounded out of bed and just reached the bathroom before the storm broke. When it was over and she was feeling a little better she noticed something for the first time.

She was wearing only a bra and panties. They were peach-coloured, flimsy lace, and might as well not have existed for all they concealed. Her golden dress and her tights had been removed.

When? Where? How?

She made her way carefully back to her room, and mercifully her mother was there with strong tea.

'Did you have too much to drink last night, dear? Andrew said you'd come over faint and asked him to bring you home, but I couldn't help wondering—well, not to worry. I could see he's a really nice young man.'

Oh, sure, he's a nice young man. He stripped me almost naked while I was unconscious. And he had the unspeakable nerve to hang my dress up neatly on a hanger.

It was there, on the wardrobe, hung and straightened by skilled hands. Its very perfection was an outrage.

'What did he tell you?' she mumbled into her tea.

'He brought you home, and when you got here you went straight to bed, and he sat downstairs waiting for us so that he could explain that you were already here, and we needn't wait up.'

'He's Johnny's elder brother.'

'He told us. Apparently he's a doctor. I always thought you liked young men to be a bit more colourful than that.'

'He's not a boyfriend. I only met him last night.'

'But he's the one you turned to when you needed help, so he must have made a big impression on you.'

'He did that, all right,' she muttered.

'It's nice to know that you're getting so discerning now you're growing up.'

That was the final insult. *'Mum!'*

'What, dear?'

'I'm seventeen. It'll be years before I'm interested in a boring doctor. He just happened to have a car.'

'You mean that revolting van? You must be really smitten if you liked him for that.'

'I'm not feeling well,' she said hastily. 'I think I'll go back to sleep.'

Her mother tactfully left her and Ellie snuggled down, feeling like a wrung-out rag. As she drifted off she remembered the stranger who'd tried to drag her away. She might have passed out with him instead of with Andrew, and instinct told her that he wouldn't have simply brought her home and put her to bed.

Try as she might she couldn't recall Andrew removing her clothes and putting her to bed. He was rude and insufferable, but he'd saved her from a nasty fate. What was more, he'd seen her almost naked, which none of her boyfriends had. It was maddening to think that he might have looked at her with admiration, and she hadn't known.

But as the waves of sleep came over her again, she began to dream. She was in a moving vehicle that stopped suddenly. The door beside her opened and she was pulled out so that she fell against a man who picked her up in his arms as easily as if she'd weighed nothing.

He was carrying her—there was the click of the front door, then the feel of climbing. It felt good to rest against him—safe and warm. Somehow her arm had found its way around his neck, her face was buried against him, and she could hear the soft thunder of his heartbeat.

They were in her room and she was being lowered gently onto the bed. His face swam in and out of her consciousness, lean, serious, the mobile features full of expression—if only she could read it.

But then the darkness obscured everything, and she was sinking down, down into deep sleep, leaving the dream and its mysteries for another time.

Her very first hangover was a grim experience, but by late afternoon she'd rejoined the human race. Soon Andrew would drop by to see how she was. Their eyes would meet, and each would see in the other's the memory of last night.

She dressed plainly in trousers and top, and applied only the very slightest make-up. This elegant restraint would make him forget the juvenile who'd aroused his scorn. He would be intrigued. They would talk and he would discover that she had a brain and a personality as well as a beautiful shape. He would become her willing slave, and that would serve him right for dismissing her as a kid.

But it wasn't Andrew who called. Only Johnny.

Rats!

'Hallo, Johnny,' she said, trying not to sound as disappointed as she felt.

'You better now? You were looking pretty green when I last saw you.'

'I wonder why,' she said pointedly.

'Yeah, right,' he mumbled. 'It was my fault. No need to keep on. I've had it all from Andrew.'

'Oh?' she said carelessly. 'What did he say?'

'What didn't he say?' Johnny struck a declamatory attitude. '"Pouring cider down the throat of a silly girl who hasn't got two brain cells to rub together—"'

'Who's he calling silly?' she demanded indignantly. This scene wasn't going to plan, but how could it when the leading man was missing?

'Why don't we go back to your home now?' she suggested casually. 'Then I can thank him.'

'He's not there. This morning he took off to visit his girlfriend.'

'*What?* How long for?'

'Dunno! Lilian's studying for medical exams too, so they'll probably work together. I'll bet they study far into the night, and then go to bed to sleep. And that's all he'll do. He's got ice water in his veins.'

As in a flash of lightning she saw Andrew's face leaning over her as he began to remove her clothes. Not ice water.

Then the lightning was gone, and she was here again with Johnny, suddenly realising how young he was. How could she ever have been flattered by the admiration of this boy?

But for the next few days she still hung around with him, had supper at his house, just in case Andrew appeared. But he didn't, and after four days she gave this up. She told Andrew's mother that she was so sorry to have missed him, and she would write him a note of thanks. Sitting at the kitchen table, she applied herself.

> Dear Andrew,
> I shall give this note to your mother, and ask her to make sure that you get it. I owe you my thanks— for the help you gave me at the party the other night.

Good. Dignified and restrained, and giving no clue to her real thoughts: *You're a dirty, rotten so-and-so for not coming to see me.*

'There are two "esses" in passionate,' said Andrew's voice over her shoulder.

She jumped with sheer astonishment. 'What—? I didn't—'

'And one "y" in undying, and one "u" in gratitude.'

She leapt up to confront him. 'What are you on about?' she demanded. She could have screamed at being caught unawares after all her careful plans. Once again life had handed her the wrong script.

But his face came out of the right script. It was tired and pale, as if he'd studied too long, but his eyes held a glowing light that made her want to smile.

'I was writing you a note to thank you for your

help, but I never said anything about passionate, undying gratitude.'

He took it from her and studied the few words regretfully. 'You just hadn't reached that bit yet,' he suggested.

'In your dreams! Just because a person is being polite, that doesn't mean that another person can go creeping up behind them and—and make fun of them—when all a person was doing was—was—'

'Being polite,' he supplied helpfully.

'I'd have thanked you myself if you'd still been around next day.'

'I thought I'd better not be,' he said quietly.

Suddenly she was growing warm, as though he'd openly referred to the way he'd undressed her. She turned away so that he shouldn't see how her cheeks were flaming.

The next moment the rest of the family entered the kitchen. There were greetings, laughter, surprise.

'I thought you were staying until the end of the week,' his mother said.

'Oh, you know me,' Andrew said carelessly. 'Always chopping and changing.'

'You? Once you've decided on something it's like arguing with a rock.'

Andrew merely gave the calm smile that Ellie was to come to know. It meant that other people's opinions washed off him.

'I feel sorry for Lilian, if she marries you,' Grace teased.

'She won't,' Andrew said mildly. 'Too much good sense.'

'Sense?' Grace echoed, aghast. 'Is that what you say about the love of your life? Don't you thrill when you see her? Doesn't your heart beat with anticipation, your pulse—?'

'Whoever invented kid sisters ought to be shot,' Andrew observed without heat.

'Who's a kid?' Grace demanded. 'I'm seventeen.'

'From where I'm standing that's a kid,' Andrew teased.

Grace took hold of Ellie's arm. 'Come on, let's go upstairs and play my new records.'

'No, let's help your mother lay the table,' Ellie said quickly. Anything was better than being bracketed with Andrew's 'kid' sister.

After the meal they all went out into the garden and watched fireflies, talking about nothing in particular. When the rest went in she hung back, touching his arm lightly so that he turned and stayed with her.

'I didn't say thank you properly,' she said.

In the darkness she could just make out his grin. 'You were saying different at the time. Nothing was bad enough for me.'

'Well—I wasn't quite myself.'

'You were smashed. Not a pretty sight. And very dangerous.'

'Yes, I might fall into the hands of a man who'd undress me while I was unconscious,' she pointed out. 'That could be dangerous too.'

She wasn't really annoyed with him for undressing her, but for some reason she wanted to talk about it.

'What are you saying? Are you asking me if I ravished you?'

She smiled at him provocatively. 'Did you?'

'Stop playing games with me, Ellie,' he said quietly. 'You're too young and ignorant about men to risk this kind of conversation.'

'Is it risky?'

'It would be with some men. It's not with me because I know how innocent you really are, and I respect it.'

'You mean I mustn't ask if you "ravished" me?'

He was angry then. 'You know damned well I didn't.'

'How do I know?'

'Because you'd know if I had.'

'So why undress me at all?'

'If I'd just dumped you into bed fully clothed your mother would have guessed that you were incapable. I was trying to make everything look as normal as possible. But I'm a doctor. I'm used to naked bodies, and yours meant nothing to me.'

She glared. It was maddening not to be able to tell him that this was just what she minded most.

Grace put her head out of the window. 'Andrew, Lilian's on the phone.'

She couldn't help overhearing the first part of the call. 'Lilian? Hi, honey, yes, I got here OK—it was a wonderful few days, wasn't it? You know I do—' He gave a soft laugh that seemed to go through Ellie.

She stood still, filled with sensations that she didn't understand and couldn't control. Andrew was a man, not a boy. He excited her and mystified her, and he had all the allure of the unknown. But her chief sensation, although she didn't understand it then, was childish, hurt pride.

There and then she made up her mind that she was going to make him fall in love with her, and that would show everyone. Above all it would show him that he couldn't look down on her from lofty heights.

Oh, God, she thought now, looking back down the tunnel of years, *I was only seventeen. What did I know?*

The house stood well back from the road, almost hidden by trees. It was large and costly, the residence of a wealthy, successful man.

It was dusk as Andrew drove up the winding drive, and there were no lights to greet him. But for himself the house was empty, and even he spent very little time here since his wife and son had departed. He had a bachelor flat near the hospital.

This grandiose place wasn't a home to him. It never had been. He'd bought it three years ago to satisfy Myra, who'd fallen in love with its size and luxury. She'd been the wife of the youngest top-ranking cardiothoracic surgeon in the country, and she'd expected to live appropriately. Andrew had demurred at the house, which was almost a mansion, with a porticoed door and walls covered with ivy. But Myra had insisted, and he'd yielded, as so often, to conceal the fact that his feeling for her had died. If it had ever lived.

For a while she'd enjoyed playing lady of the manor. She'd named the place 'Oaks' after the two magnificent trees in the garden. She'd bought their son, Simon, a pony, and had him taught to ride in the grounds. But by that time their marriage had effectively been over. She hadn't even wanted Oaks as part of the divorce settlement.

He was pouring himself a drink when his mobile went. It was Myra, which made his head immediately start to ache.

'You're no easier to get hold of than you ever were,' she said wryly. 'Where are you?'

'The house.'

'What are you rattling around in that place for?'

'I can't think.'

'Just checking about the weekend. Simon's looking forward to seeing you.'

'Look, I was going to call you about that—'

'Don't you dare!'

'I'll have to work over the weekend. Can't you explain to Simon, make him understand?'

'But he already does understand, Andrew. It's *what* he understands that should be worrying you. He understands that he's always last on your list of priorities.'

'That's not true.'

'Damn, it *is* true! Look, I married you knowing your work always came first. I made that choice. But Simon didn't. He expects to have a father who loves him—'

'Don't dare say I don't love my son,' he barked.

'Do you think I need to say it? Don't you think he knows it every time you let him down?'

'Put him on.'

The talk with his son was a disaster. Simon was quiet and polite, saying, 'Yes, Daddy,' and 'It's all right, Daddy,' at regular intervals. And it wasn't all right. It was all dreadfully wrong, and he didn't know what to do about it.

He was tired to the bone. He microwaved something from the freezer, barely noticing what it was, then settled down in front of his computer. For two hours he worked mechanically and only stopped because his head was aching too badly for him to think. But that was good. He didn't want to think.

He wondered why he suddenly felt so drained and

futile. The demands of work were crushing, but they always were. Pressure, stress, instant decisions, life and death—these were the things he thrived on, without which he wouldn't exist. Suddenly they weren't enough. Or rather, they were too much. For the first time in his career—no, his whole life—he wondered if he could cope with everything that was required of him.

It was absurd to connect this sudden loss of confidence with the brief moment in the hospital corridor when he'd been confronted with a past he'd thought safely dead and buried.

Buried. Not dead.

He hunted in the top drawer of his desk until he found a set of keys, selected one, and used it to open the bottom drawer. At the back, buried under a pile of papers, was an envelope, stuffed with photographs. He laid it on the desk, but made no move to open it, as though reluctant to take the final step.

At last he shook out the contents onto the desk, and spread them out with one hand. They were cheap snaps, nothing special, except for the glowing faces of the two young people in them.

The girl's long blonde hair streamed over her shoulders in glorious profusion, her face was brilliant with life. It was that life, rather than her beauty, that made her striking. All youth and abundance seemed to have gathered in her, as though any man who came near her must be touched by her golden shadow, and be blessed all his days.

Blessed all his days. There was a thought to bring a bitter smile to the face of a man who'd felt that blessing, and seen it die.

He lingered over the girl's laughing face, trying to

reconcile it with the weary look he'd seen on the woman in the corridor. Just once her gaze was turned on the young man, and he studied her expression, trying to detect in it some trace of the love he'd once believed in. In every other picture she was looking directly at the camera.

By contrast, the man had eyes only for her, as though nothing else in the world existed for him. His hands were about her waist or on her shoulder, touching her face, his expression one of tender adoration.

Andrew wanted to seize him, shake him, crying, You fool, don't be taken in by her. She's nothing but a cold-hearted little schemer, who'll break your heart and laugh at you.

She'd been laughing when he'd first seen her at the party, dancing with blissful abandon. With her head thrown back in enjoyment, her eyes sparkling, she'd seemed the very embodiment of everything he'd given up on the day he'd decided to be the greatest doctor in the world. He'd devoted himself to study, ignoring the young, heedless pleasures that other medical students had seemed to find time for. They'd been all right for people who'd been satisfied with being ordinary doctors, but he hadn't been satisfied, and he hadn't been going to be ordinary.

Without warning this shimmering pixie had burst on him, and before he'd been able to control the feeling, he'd been filled with fierce regret for the whole side of life he'd rejected. He'd escaped to the kitchen, away from the sight of her.

But then she'd appeared, looking even younger close-up, and he'd known that she'd been dangerous to his peace of mind. He'd assumed an air of lofty indifference, talking to her with one eye still on his book, as though he hadn't been able to tear himself away, although the truth had been that every fibre of him had been aware of her.

He'd have liked to believe her claim of being nineteen, but her air of bravado had given her away. She'd flirted like a kid, crossing her beautiful legs on the table near him, and saying she liked older men in a 'come hither' voice that would have finished him but for his stern resolutions. His advice to 'go back to your party, pretty little girl' had been an act of desperation.

He'd promised himself to avoid her, but when he'd seen boys getting her drunk for a laugh he'd had to step in and rescue her.

He'd taken the house key from her purse and carried her up the stairs to what he'd guessed had been her room. He'd removed her clothes because if her mother had found her fully dressed and asleep she might have guessed the truth. He was a doctor, and impersonal, so he'd thought.

But he'd found himself holding a girl wearing a bra and panties so wispy as to have been almost non-existent. Laying her gently on the bed, he'd been shocked to find how his hands had longed to linger over her silky skin and perfect shape. He'd hung up her dress, using the controlled movements to impose discipline on his mind and, through his mind, his sensations. Discipline, control, order. That was how it had always been with him.

But not this time. Fear had seized him, and he'd got out as fast as he'd been able to.

He'd fled to the imagined safety of Lilian, a girlfriend as sedate and studious as himself. But there had been no safety there, or anywhere. After that it was too late. It had always been too late.

CHAPTER THREE

HETTA and Elinor shared their cramped little room both night and day. It meant that Elinor spent half her night listening for Hetta's breathing, terrified lest her child had slipped away in the darkness. Each dawn she gave thanks that Hetta was still alive, and tried to convince herself that she wasn't losing ground. Every morning she went to work and telephoned home after the first hour, to hear Daisy say, 'She's fine.' In the late afternoon she hurried home at the first chance, anxious to look at Hetta's face and lie to herself that the little girl wasn't really looking paler or more tired.

There were the regular check-ups with the local doctor, who assured her that Hetta was 'holding on'. And there were the further check-ups at the hospital, where Sir Elmer Rylance would make kindly noises.

'I promise you Hetta is top of the list,' he told her once. 'As soon as a suitable heart becomes available...'

But day followed day, week followed week, and no heart ever became available.

If it ever did happen she knew she would be called at home, yet she couldn't help a glimmer of hope as she and Hetta entered the cardiac unit for their April appointment. It was two months since she'd last been here and glimpsed Andrew Blake from a distance. In that time she'd managed to persuade herself that she'd imagined it.

There was a new nurse today, young and not very

confident. She ushered Elinor and Hetta into the consulting room and seemed taken aback to find it empty.

'Oh, yes,' the nurse said quickly, 'I should have told you—'

'It's all right,' came a man's voice from the door. 'I'll explain everything to Mrs Landers.'

She knew the voice at once, just as she had recognised his face, despite the years. As he closed the door behind the nurse and went to the desk Elinor waited for him to look at her, braced herself for the shock in his eyes.

'I apologise for Sir Elmer's absence, Mrs Landers,' he said briskly. 'I'm afraid he's gone down with a touch of flu. My name is Andrew Blake, and I'm taking over his appointments for today.'

He looked up, shook hands with her briefly, and returned to his notes.

He didn't recognise her.

After the first shock she felt an overwhelming relief. Only Hetta mattered. She had no time for distractions.

He talked to the child in a gentle, unemotional voice, listened to her heart, and asked questions. He didn't talk down to her, Elinor was impressed to see, but assumed that she understood a good deal. Hetta didn't disappoint him. She was an old hand at this by now.

'Do you get breathless more often than you used to?' he asked.

Hetta nodded and made a face. 'It's a pig.'

'I'm sure it is. I expect there's lots you can't do.'

'Heaps and heaps,' she said, sensing a sympathetic ear. 'I want a dog, but Mummy says it would be too bois—something.'

'Too boisterous,' Andrew agreed.

'Hetta, that's not really the reason,' Elinor protested. 'We can't have pets in that little room.'

'You live in one room?' Andrew asked.

'In a boarding house. It's just a bit tiny, but everyone's fond of Hetta and kind to her.'

'Do you smoke?'

'No. I never did, but I wouldn't do it around Hetta.'

'Good. What about the other tenants?'

'Mr Jenson smokes like a chimney,' Hetta confided. 'Daisy's very cross with him.'

'Tell me about the others.'

Man and child became absorbed in their talk, giving Elinor the opportunity to watch him, and note the changes of twelve years.

He had always been a tall man, slightly too thin for his height. Now that he'd filled out he was imposing. Perhaps his face had grown sharper, his chin a little more forceful, but he still had a thick shock of dark hair with no sign of thinning. At thirty-eight he was the essence of power and success, exactly as he'd always meant to be.

At last he said, 'Hetta, do you know the play area just along the corridor?'

'Mmm! They've got a rabbit,' she said wistfully.

'Would you like to go along and see the rabbit now?'

Hetta nodded and left the room as eagerly as her constant weariness would allow.

'Is there anyone to help you with her?' Andrew asked. 'Family?'

'My parents are both dead. Daisy helps me a lot. She's the landlady, and like a second mother to me. She cares for Hetta when I'm out working.'

'Is your job very demanding?'

'I'm a freelance beautician. I go into people's homes to do their hair, nails and make-up. It has the advantage that I can make my own hours.'

'But if you have to take time off you don't get paid, I suppose.'

'It will be different when she's well. Then I can work really hard and make some money to take her away for a holiday. We talk about that—' She stopped, her voice running down wearily. Why was she telling him these unlikely dreams that would never come true?

Now she was passionately glad that he hadn't recognised her as he listened to her tale of defeat and failure.

'Is Hetta any worse?' she asked desperately.

'There's been some slight deterioration but nothing to be too troubled about. I've made a small change in her medication,' he said, scribbling. 'It'll make her breathing a little easier. Call my office if you're alarmed about her condition.'

I'm always alarmed about her condition, she wanted to scream. *I'm alarmed, terrified, despairing. and you can't help. You were going to be the world's greatest doctor, but my child is dying and you can't do anything.*

But all she said was, 'Thank you.'

'Good day to you, Mrs Landers.'

'Good day.'

That night, as always, she sat with Hetta. When the child had fallen asleep she rose and went to the window, looking out onto the unlovely back yards that were so typical of this depressing neighbourhood.

A machine, she thought. *That's what he's become.*

*Just a machine. It was always bound to happen. Even
back then he had his life planned out, a straight path,
dead ahead, and no distractions to the left or the
right. He said so.*

*Why did I ever worry? I didn't make any impact
on him. Not in the end.*

It had been so simple to promise herself that she
would win Andrew's heart. But as week had followed
week in silence she'd faced the fact that he'd returned
to Lilian and forgotten her. She'd pictured them together, laughing about her.

'You should have seen this silly little kid I met,'
he must have said. 'Thought she was grown up, but
didn't have a clue.'

He might have telephoned to see how she was, but
he didn't.

She could have screamed. How could she make
him fall in love with her if he wasn't there?

For lack of anything better to do, she continued
going out with the kids in the gang, although after
Andrew their conversation sounded juvenile, and their
concerns meaningless. The boys talked about the
girls, the girls sighed over pop stars and made eyes
at the boys. The talk was mildly indecent in an ignorant sort of way.

Then Jack Smith appeared among them. He was a
motor mechanic, brashly handsome, and twenty-one.
He fixed on Ellie as the best-looking girl in town, and
his admiration, following Andrew's departure,
warmed her.

'A smasher, that's what you are,' he told her one
night when they were all sitting at a table outside a
pub. 'Bet you could have any feller you wanted.'

'She could,' Grace agreed. 'You should have seen her at our birthday party. They were all over her. Even Andrew.'

'No, he wasn't,' Ellie's honesty compelled her to say. 'He was saving me from the others.'

'Oh, go on! What happened when he got you alone? You've never told.'

'And I'm never going to.'

There were knowing cries of 'Ooh!'

'Who is this Andrew?' Jack demanded.

'My snooty elder brother,' Grace said. 'He carried Ellie out of the party thrown over his shoulder, like a caveman.'

'No, he didn't,' Ellie corrected. 'He just lifted me off the floor a bit.'

'But he'd have *liked* to throw you over his shoulder, wouldn't he?'

Ellie would have given a lot to know the answer to that question herself.

'Bet he fancies you really,' Grace persisted.

'Don't think so,' Ellie said, clinging onto truthfulness with a touch of desperation. It was hard because her pride was involved. 'Don't forget about Lilian.'

'Bet you could make him forget Lilian,' Grace nagged. 'Bet you could if you set your mind to it.'

'Ellie could make *anyone* fall in love with her,' Jack said admiringly. 'Whether she had a mind to or not.'

'Not Andrew,' Ellie said, to bring the conversation back to him. 'Nobody will ever get under his skin.'

'Bet you could,' Grace obliged.

'Bet I couldn't,' Ellie said, speaking gruffly to hide how much the thought pleased her.

'Bet you could.'

'Bet I couldn't.'

'Could.'

'Couldn't.'

'Could.'

'Couldn't!'

In the end she shrugged and said, 'Well, maybe I could if I set my mind to it. But I'm not going to.'

'Oh, go on! It'll be fun seeing my big brother when he's not being so cocky.'

'Yes,' Ellie murmured with feeling.

'Go on, then.'

'No.'

'You're chicken.'

'I'm not.'

'You are.'

'I'm not.'

'You are.'

Goaded, she said, 'Listen, I could have anyone I want, and that includes your snooty brother. But I'm not interested in him.'

'So pretend.'

'I'll think about it.'

Like children squabbling in the playground, she thought, years later. *That was the level of the conversation that had ultimately broken a man's heart.*

Even as a child Andrew had been orderly about remembering dates and details. For a man of science it was very useful.

But there were times he would have been glad of a little forgetfulness. His brother's birthday, for instance, which came exactly seven weeks and three days after Grace's birthday party; seven weeks and three days after the night he'd met Ellie; seven weeks and two days since he'd fled her, six weeks and five days since he'd returned home to find her there and known that it had been useless to run and a mistake to return.

It would be an even worse mistake to attend Johnny's birthday festivities and risk another meeting. But his mother said it was his family duty, and duty was something Andrew never shirked.

When the day came he set out, armed with a gift for his brother, but as he reached town it occurred to him to buy something for his mother too, and headed for the nearest department store.

And there was Ellie, serving on the cosmetics counter, laughing with a customer as she demonstrated a perfume on her wrist. She didn't see Andrew at first, so that he had time to stand and watch her. And in that moment he knew that all the discipline and control, all the mental tricks to blot her out, had been for nothing, and the truth was that he had thought of her night and day since their last meeting.

She looked up and saw him. Smiled. He smiled back. It was all over.

When the customer had gone he approached her, heart thumping. To cover his confusion he made his face sterner and more rigid than usual.

'Good morning,' he said, almost fiercely.

'Hey, don't bite my head off,' she protested, laughing. 'What have I done wrong?'

'Nothing,' he said hastily. 'I only said good morning.'

'You made it sound like the crack of doom.'

Her smile touched him again, and this time he relaxed a little. 'I'm looking for something for my mother,' he told her. 'I don't see why Johnny should have all the gifts.'

'Johnny?'

'His nineteenth birthday.'

'Is it? I didn't know.'

'But aren't you coming to the party?' he asked, dismayed.

'I haven't seen much of Johnny lately,' she said with a light shrug. 'Do you want perfume, or lipstick, or——?'

'Pardon?'

'For your mother.'

'My mother? Oh, yes, her present.'

Pull yourself together, he thought. *You're burbling like an idiot.*

'What sort of make-up does she wear?' Ellie asked.

'Um...' He looked at her, wild-eyed, and she laughed at his confusion. But not unkindly.

'I'll bet you've never noticed if she wears any at all,' she teased.

'It's not the sort of thing I'm good at,' he confessed.

'You and the rest of the male population.'

'What do you do for the others?'

'Scented soap is pretty safe, especially with some nice gift wrapping.'

She showed him a variety of boxed soaps and he chose the biggest, an astounding pink and mauve creation.

'I thought you'd pick that one,' she said.

'I guess that means everyone does, huh?'

'Not everyone. Only the fellers. I'll gift-wrap it for free. I guess I owe you, and I like to pay my debts.'

'Ah! Now that's a pity because I was hoping you'd pay your debt in another way.'

'How?'

'I'd feel self-conscious turning up alone at this do. Since you and Johnny are—aren't—well, you might come with me. Just to make me look good.'

'You didn't bring Lilian?'

'Why should you ask that?' he demanded, suddenly self-conscious. 'It's what my mother said. I don't know why everyone assumes that—I'm fond of Lilian but we're not joined at the hip—head—' he corrected hastily. He had a horrible feeling that he was blushing like a boy.

'The only problem is that it's the store's late night,' Ellie said. 'We don't close until nine.'

'I'll be outside, waiting.'

When the time came she was late, filling him with dread lest she'd thought better of it and stood him up.

'Did you think I wasn't coming?' Her voice burst through his gloomy reverie. 'I'm so sorry, but the manager wouldn't stop talking.'

'It doesn't matter,' he said, brilliant with joy. 'You're here.'

She tucked her arm in his as they began to walk. 'Have you been to Johnny's party?'

'Yes, and it was noisy. Johnny was talking about going to the funfair in the park later, and most of the food at home has gone now. Why don't we grab a snack somewhere, and join them later?'

'Great.'

He took her to a small French restaurant, formal, but pleasantly quiet. She didn't look out of place here as she would have done in her gold party get-up,

Andrew realised. Everything about her was more restrained, more gentle, more delightful.

'Did your mother like her present?' she asked.

'She was over the moon,' he said truthfully. 'You'd have thought I'd bought her a whole bath house instead of a few cakes of soap.'

'It's not the soap. It's because you thought of her.'

'I guess you're right.'

'I know I'm right. You should see some of my male customers, getting all worked up about this perfume or that perfume, treating it like rocket science. And I want to grab their lapels and yell, ''Just show her you've thought of her. That's the real present.'' Gee, men can be so dumb.'

'I guess we can,' he said, entranced, willing her to go on.

She did so, entertaining him for several minutes with a witty description of life at the cosmetics counter, which seemed to be a crash course in human nature. Again he had the feeling that she was more mature than he remembered. The true reason didn't occur to him. This was her subject. She was an expert in it, and therefore at an advantage.

She was a joy to treat, revelling in every new taste with a defenceless candour that went to his heart.

'You aren't eating,' she challenged, looking up from the steak dressed with the chef's 'special' sauce.

'I'm enjoying watching you too much,' he said, and was surprised at himself. Normally he avoided any remark, however trivial, that savoured of self-revelation. It was her, he decided. Her frankness demanded a response.

'It's yummy,' she said blissfully.

'And there's even better to come.'

'Ice cream?'

'That's right. We'll have everything on the menu.'

'Go on, I'm more grown up than that.' She looked at him slyly. 'Well, almost.'

He groaned. 'Am I ever going to be forgiven for the things I said that time?'

'Well, I guess you were right. Mind you, I'd die before admitting it.'

He grinned. She laughed back, and suddenly their first meeting became a shared joke.

'I'm surprised you want to bother with a kids' party,' she said. 'Don't we all seem very juvenile to you?'

'My mother wanted me to come, and I guess I did it to please her.'

'That was kind of you. Like the soap.'

Again he knew the unfamiliar impulse to frankness. After resisting for a moment he yielded and found it unexpectedly easy. 'Not really,' he said. 'Part of me's trying to ease my conscience for being a bad son.'

'A bad son? You? No way. Your mother's terribly proud of you, all you've achieved—top marks in all your exams, really going places.'

'But in a sense I've done it at her expense, or at the expense of the family, which is the same thing. You can only give all of yourself to one thing at a time. I've held back from my family and given myself to work, which is something that benefits me, first and most.'

'But what about the people you heal? You benefit them. If you were only concerned about yourself you could be a banker or—or anything that makes a lot of money.'

'But I'd have been a terrible banker and I'm a good

doctor. It makes sense to play to my skills. And by the time I've finished I'll have made a lot of money. But I have to be the best. And I will, whatever the cost.'

He'd gone further than he'd meant to. She was staring at him.

'You really mean that, don't you?'

'Do I sound very cold-blooded? Should I have talked about my mission to do good?'

She shook her head. 'People with missions to do good scare me. They always want to tell other people what to do. As long as you make sick people well, who cares about your reasons?'

'That's what I think,' he said, feeling a load slip away from him at finding someone who understood.

Suddenly he was talking, telling her about the frustrations of his childhood when he'd dreamed of escaping this dull little town where his parents had lived their contented lives.

'They're happy, and that's fine for them, but this place couldn't be enough for me.'

'What would be enough?'

'The top.'

'But which tree? You're working in a hospital now, aren't you?'

'That's right. Long hours, low pay. It's backbreaking and you don't get any sleep. No matter. It's great. I'm learning, and I'll get there.'

'And what then?'

'Then? Then I'll have everything I want.'

He knew, even as he said it, that it couldn't be true unless 'everything' included her. But he shied from the thought. It wasn't in the plan.

'I suppose we ought to put in an appearance at the funfair,' he said.

'Ooh, yes,' she said, becoming young again.

They went on everything, the scenic railway, the dodgems, the carousel, the big wheel. The wheel scared her and he had to put his arm around her. Then she forgot her fear and laughed up into his face, so that everything vanished, leaving just the two of them high up above the world.

And that was when he kissed her, with the stars raining about them and the sound of fireworks all around. He didn't know if the fireworks were real or inside himself, but they glittered and sparkled as she threw her arms about his neck and gave him back kiss for kiss.

'I've been plotting for ages how to kiss you,' he said when they freed their lips, gasping. 'And I'm such a coward that I waited until now, when you can't escape.'

'I don't want to escape,' she said recklessly. 'Kiss me—kiss me—'

He kissed her again and again, revelling in the response he could feel in her eager young body, and promising himself—chivalrous idiot that he was—not to abuse her trust.

Looking back down the years to that night, Andrew judged his young self harshly.

Fool. Bird brain. No common sense, or if you had you'd put it on hold. She was playing with you, laughing at you, and you fell for it like a daft boy, because you wanted to believe all those pretty fairy tales, and that's the stupidest thing of all.

But sometimes he would sigh and murmur, 'Just the same, I was a better man then than I am now.'

CHAPTER FOUR

AT SEVENTEEN Ellie reckoned life should be fun, and romance was part of that fun. You played the field, and if you won the man you'd set your heart on that was wonderful, but there were still other men in the world.

Of course she was crazy about Andrew—for the moment. They would date, and love each other; she would find a job in the same town as his hospital.

But she was startled to discover that his feelings were of a different order. He was a serious, dedicated man in his love as in his work. He offered her total commitment and he demanded the same in return.

Away from him Ellie made firm resolutions about cooling their relationship, refusing to let him make plans for their future. But with him her plans melted in the intensity of his adoration.

'Darling, darling, Ellie, you do love me, don't you?'

And as she looked into his glowing eyes the only possible answer was yes.

He never actually asked her to marry him, simply started talking about it as a foregone conclusion. Her mother was thrilled that she'd found 'a nice, steady young man' so soon, and she didn't know how to tell Mum that Andrew's steadiness was a point against him.

She was flattered, overwhelmed, confused, ecstatic, filled with love, longing and desire. The depth of his feelings touched her heart and made her tender towards him, which increased his love. It was all sweet and wonderful, but down the end of the rose strewn tunnel she saw dirty plates, dirty socks, dirty nappies.

'What's wrong with having children while we're young?' he asked when she managed to voice some doubts.

'Because it's not how I want to spend my youth,' she flung back. 'I want a career first.'

'Darling, one day I'm going to be a top consultant. I don't want my wife doing shampoos and sets.'

'Why you—you dinosaur!' she exploded.

Soon they were in the middle of a blazing row, their first. Ellie was upset, but Andrew was torn apart. His misery shocked her and she flung herself into his arms, longing only to comfort him. Making up was blissful, but afterwards she was more firmly tied to him than ever, and she was beginning to feel like a prisoner.

Yet she couldn't break away. He filled her with bittersweet emotions that she'd never known before, so intense that it was like living in a new, glowing world. She could only cling on and hope for a miracle to make everything right.

His mother was appalled at the prospect of his early marriage to a girl who could bring him no advantages. 'You could do a great deal better for yourself,' she snapped in Ellie's presence.

But Andrew slipped his arm about his beloved's shoulder, drawing her close to his tall, strong body, and said gently, 'She loves me, as much as I love her. Could I do better than that?' Then his voice rose joyfully. 'Mum, be happy for me. I've got the most wonderful girl in the world.'

She wanted him, ached for him, and raged at the old-fashioned chivalry that made him refuse until they were married. She guessed that her youth preyed on his mind, but she knew too little of the world to respect his strength of will and consideration for her. She only felt that she wanted to be naked with him, make love to him, please him and be pleased by him. Her body was beautiful, but he would do nothing to claim her. It was insulting.

Since they had no money they spent their time together wandering in the park where the funfair had been. One day they took a boat out onto the lake. The weather was hot, and Andrew wore only a pair of shorts. She lay back blissfully and watched the sun turning his skin to gold as he pulled on the oars, making nothing of the task.

She thought of his strength, how she'd sensed it through his kisses, the movements of his hands, both tender and urgent. She knew he desired her and was fighting it. But how long could he hold out against his own feelings?

They pulled into a little island where they could picnic in a secluded spot under the trees. Afterwards she lay in the crook of his arm, listening to his heartbeat.

'Do you love me?' she whispered.

He raised himself, pushing her down onto the blanket and looking down on her. 'How can you ask me that?' he said in a quiet, serious voice. 'Don't you know by now how much I love you? Don't you know that you fill the world for me?'

She reached up and touched his face with her fingertips, trying to smooth away the frown lines that hard work and study were already etching on his face.

Slowly she worked her hands around to the back of his head and drew him down until his lips touched hers. Instantly she was afire, filled with need and longing. She pressed against him, kissing him back eagerly, fiercely, willing him to abandon himself to feeling and sensation.

To her delight she could sense it happening. He touched her like a man on the verge of losing control, caressing her face, her neck, her breasts through the thin cotton of her blouse. Where his fingers touched, his lips followed, burning her with their passion and satisfying her deeply. She gasped at the flickering of fire that went across her skin, making every inch of her newly aware.

She ran her hands over his bare back, feeling lean, hard muscles, sensing his strength. She wanted to kiss him everywhere.

He fumbled at the buttons of her blouse and she helped him, freeing her breasts to his adoring gaze. His lips against them sent shudders of delight through her, and then again when the tip of his tongue caressed one peaked nipple.

'Andrew,' she whispered, 'darling, yes—please…'

He was fumbling at the waistband of her shorts, opening the button, drawing down the zipper, slipping his hand lovingly inside to where she was eager for him. In another few moments, she thought blissfully, she would know what love was really all about, and then—

She opened her eyes to find him staring at her with shock. There was no desire on his face, only horror, like a man who'd awakened from a nightmare.

'What is it?' she whispered.

'Dear God, what am I doing?' he said hoarsely. 'I promised myself—'

He drew away and jumped to his feet. The next moment he'd taken to his heels and fled.

'Andrew!' she screamed.

But he kept on running as though the devil were after him. She buried her face in her hands, racked by sobs of frustration and rejection.

She was still weeping when he returned a few minutes later. The sight made him fling himself down beside her, taking her in his arms and murmuring words of love and tenderness.

'Ellie, darling, forgive me. I never meant to make you cry, but I couldn't go on,' he said desperately.

'But *why*?' she cried in a shaking voice.

'Because I want you too much, can't you understand that?'

'No! How can you want me too much if you say you love me? It's all a lie, isn't it? You don't really love me at all.'

He became angry. 'Is that how love looks to you? A man has to grab you selfishly, take what he wants and to hell with you, before you can believe he loves you?'

'But it wouldn't be to hell with me because I want it too.'

'What are you telling me? That I wouldn't be the first?' This was a new Andrew, his face dark with possessiveness. What was his was his.

'No, I'm not saying that,' she cried, losing her temper. 'How dare you?'

'I'm sorry, I didn't mean it. Ellie, please let's not quarrel.'

'If you loved me you'd want to make love to me,' she wept.

'And I do want to make love to you. Hell, if you knew how badly I want that! But not like this, out in the open where someone might come along. A quickie after lunch, as though you were some cheap floozie. I think better of you than that and you should think better of yourself.'

'Stop preaching at me,' she cried. 'Everything I want is wrong according to you. You want to make me old before my time.'

'I want to make you happy,' he said miserably. 'But I'm making a rotten job of it. Forgive me for hurting you.'

That was how it was between them. He was a hard, stubborn man, unshakeable in his resolve to do what he saw was right. She could break herself to bits against that rock. Yet the depth and intensity of his love were such that of the two it was he who was her slave, not the other way around. He wouldn't yield, but he would be the first to apologise.

They made it up, after a fashion. But this time the reconciliation was different, tinged with caution. They had learned how they could hurt each other.

Jack Smith was still hanging around, ignoring Ellie's engagement.

'You won't marry him,' he told her once. 'You want a bloke who knows how to enjoy life, like me.'

She was feeling especially sore with Andrew just then, for his stick-in-the-mud attitudes, and she smiled brilliantly at Jack, and didn't deny.

After that he was often around, always available to escort her when Andrew was away working. One day

Andrew turned up unexpectedly and found them having a drink together.

'Don't be stuffy,' she cried, when he complained later.

'Either you're my girl or you're not!'

'Maybe I'm not if you're going to put me on a ball and chain.'

'He's a bad lot, Ellie. Even you should be able to see that.'

'What do you mean, even me?'

'You know what I mean.'

'No, tell me.'

'Someone without two thoughts to rub together,' he snapped in one of his rare flares of temper.

'Then I'm surprised you want to marry me.'

His face had softened. 'Because I love you more than I can say. Sometimes I wish I didn't, but I can't help it.'

She too melted. 'You don't need to be jealous of Jack, honest.'

'Jealous of that beefy idiot!' he exploded. 'Don't make me laugh.'

Perhaps they should have quarrelled properly and left it there. But a week later he arrived with plans.

'I can get two weeks off in August, darling. It can be our honeymoon.'

'But that's next month,' she gasped. Suddenly the socks and nappies had come awfully close, and she could almost see the prison bars.

Was that why she did it? How consciously did she decide to go out in the boat with Jack, to land on the same little island that she'd been with Andrew? Did she secretly know that Jack's idea of a joke would be to push the boat out into the water, so that they were stranded?

Andrew arrived the day before their wedding to find her missing. How accusing his eyes were when she and Jack were finally rescued, after being on the island all night! She faced him in her mother's house, defiant.

'It was an accident, that's all.'

'Was it an accident that you went out there? What did you mean by going with him just before our wedding, anyway?'

'I wanted to enjoy myself. No crime in that.'

'That depends how you wanted to enjoy yourself.'

'What do you mean by that?'

'You know what I mean. We went there once ourselves, and I remember your idea of enjoying yourself. But I wouldn't oblige, would I? I was thinking of you, but I don't think that ever got through to you. Was he any more co-operative?'

How cold and dead his face was, as she'd never seen it before. He'd adored her, worshipped her. Now he was close to hating her.

She could have handled it differently, told him that she'd boxed Jack's ears and forced him to keep his distance, which was the truth. And they would have made it up, and married next day.

Instead she'd defied him. 'Believe what you like. If you don't trust me, that's your problem.'

'Ellie, *darling*—' he was still hers if she wanted '—I want to trust you, but you were there all night with him. Just tell me nothing happened.'

'What do *you* think happened?'

'Tell me!'

'Leave me alone,' she screamed. 'Stop pressurising

me. Stop trying to control my life, and telling me what to do. You've got it all planned, we marry this week, we have a baby next year, and I sit at home alone with a screaming kid while you work all hours trying to become the great doctor.'

'But we agreed—'

'You agreed. You decided, you told me and I was supposed to fall in line. I don't like being bullied—'

'*I bullied you?*' Suddenly he was a sick man, his face the colour of death. 'Is that all my love meant to you? Bullying?'

'You don't let me breathe. You've got my life planned out for me, but I want something more.'

'Oh, yes, shampoos and make-up,' he snapped.

'You can sneer, but it's my choice. I don't want to live in a backwater. I want to go to London and work in a big store, and be someone.'

'And you think you're going to be someone with a pig like Jack Smith?'

'He may be a pig to you but he believes in me—'

'He's probably hoping.that you'll support him.'

'And he knows how to give a girl a good time.'

'Tell me about that good time,' he said dangerously.

'What do you want to know?' said a voice from the doorway. It was Jack, who'd forced his way past her mother and heard the last words.

'Nothing from you,' Andrew snapped. 'Get out of here.'

'No way. I'm part of this. I didn't have to force Ellie to come with me. She needed a rest from you preaching at her. I just provided the light entertainment, didn't I, darling? Very appreciative she was, too.'

The next moment he was on the floor, knocked down by a punch like a hammer. Ellie screamed, not for Jack but for Andrew, who yearned to be a surgeon but had risked his valuable right hand.

'Don't,' she begged him.

'Protecting him, Ellie?'

'No, your hand.'

'Do you think I care about that now?'

Jack had climbed to his feet, an ugly look in his eyes. She thought he was going to punch Andrew back, but he did something much worse.

'C'mon, sweetie, let's go. You won your bet, you don't have to take it to the line.'

'Bet? What bet?' Andrew asked.

'Nothing,' she said hurriedly. A pit was opening at her feet.

'Tell me about this bet,' Andrew said quietly.

'Ellie bet a whole gang of us that she could make you fall in love with her. Boy, was that a laugh! It's been an even bigger laugh watching her at work.'

Andrew looked at her. 'You—did that?'

'No—' she said desperately.

'Are you saying it's not true?'

'No—that is—not like that—'

'You mean the answer's yes?'

'It wasn't like that. Just a silly joke—'

'Don't tell me any more,' he said in a quiet voice that was worse to her than shouting. 'I really only have myself to blame for loving you too much. I should never have lost my sense of proportion. Always a mistake, that.'

'Andrew, please listen to me,' she screamed. 'Let me explain—'

'Explain what? You never really wanted to marry

me, did you, Ellie? Now I understand. After you'd made a fool of me there was nowhere else to take it. The trouble is I never had much sense of humour, although with you—' He checked, and a spasm of pain went over his face. 'Well, a lot of things were different with you.'

She'd flinched to see hate in his eyes, but now there was something far more terrible than hate. Disillusion.

'I apologise for wasting so much of your time,' he said politely, 'and also for boring you. I won't do so any longer. I wish you every happiness for the future. Good day to you.'

He walked out with a face of stone.

The following month she ran away to London with Jack Smith. They had a hurried marriage in a shabby register office and after that, as Andrew had foretold, she found herself supporting him. From then on nothing went right for her.

Elinor had awaited the call for so long that when it came one evening she didn't, at first, take it in.

'What—what did you say?'

'This is the Burdell Hospital. We have a heart which would seem to be suitable for your daughter.'

'You've got—?'

'I must caution you not to get your hopes up too high. We need to do some final tests before a decision can be made, but an ambulance is heading for you, so will you—?'

Elinor barely heard the rest. Tears of relief poured down her face. She was shaking so hard that she could hardly move, but she forced herself to be calm as she went to find Hetta, even managing a brilliant smile as she called out, 'All right, darling, we're on our way.'

'Really, Mummy? 'Cos last time—'

'I know,' Elinor said quickly. This had happened twice before and their hopes had soared, but in the end the operation hadn't been possible. 'Let's just cross our fingers.'

In no time at all the ambulance was at the door. The news had spread through the boarding house and everyone who was at home came to wave them off. Daisy flapped about like a mother hen, pouring out concern and criticism alike.

'Call me as soon as you know anything, love. Night or day. Jerry, I hope you went to the Job Centre, today. How are you, my pet? Have you got everything? Where's Samson?'

'Here,' Hetta said, producing a disreputable object that had started life as a bear.

'That's fine, then. Elinor, you tell me if there's anything I can do for you. Anything at all.'

During the short journey to the hospital she and Hetta held hands tightly. There were no words for their shared thoughts, but they didn't need words. And then they were there, and nurses were coming to meet them, smiling, looking hopeful.

Cling to that hope, she thought. *Don't think about the other chance.*

There were questions to answer. A nurse took Hetta's temperature, which was normal. Her current state of health was good.

Except that she's dying.

'I know Sir Elmer hasn't been well,' Elinor said. 'Is he back yet?'

'No, it'll be Mr Blake doing this. He's on his way in now.'

'Can I be with Hetta?'

'Just another few minutes while we finish the tests, then I'll take you in. If you could just wait here—'

That was the worst. Waiting. Walking up and down in the featureless waiting room, trying to look into the future and seeing only a blank. Up and down. Back and forth. Look out of the window into the darkness. Watch her own face shadowed in the window, then the door opening, and another presence in the room. A handsome man in a dinner jacket and black bow-tie, who'd obviously been called away from a pleasant evening.

'Have you got the answer yet?' she demanded harshly, swinging around to face him. 'Can you do it?'

'I'll be getting the results in a minute,' Andrew said. 'But please try not to worry.'

'Try not to worry,' she echoed in anguish. 'Do you know how many doctors have said that to me, and how little it means?'

'I can imagine.'

'This has happened before. Twice. The first time they called us and we rushed to the hospital, but when we got there they'd decided to give it to someone else.'

'That means your daughter was strong enough to stand the wait and the other child wasn't,' Andrew said quietly.

'I know. I rationalised it all the way home. So did Hetta. She's so grown up, and she shouldn't have to be. She kept saying, ''Never mind, Mummy. There's next time.'' And three months later it happened again.

This time there was no other candidate but there was a delay in getting the heart there, and by the time it arrived it was unusable. Has the heart arrived yet?'

'No.'

Her voice rose. 'Then it could happen again?'

'Not a chance. It's only coming a few miles.'

'But when it gets here you've got to test it and there might be something wrong—'

'Very unlikely. The other hospital does its own tests and we only hear about the heart when they're satisfied. Mrs. Landers, I know this is very hard, but I'm sure it was explained to you that these false dawns are, sadly, very common. I have patients who were called in five times before all the conditions were right for them. But it did happen in the end. They had successful transplants and now they're healthy. Hetta's chances are still good.'

'Are they? She's a child, they're much harder to match.' Elinor gave a wan smile. 'You see how much I've had time to learn.'

'I know,' he said, speaking gently. 'I know. But please try not to think the worst. I promise you, things are looking hopeful.'

She searched his face to see if he were merely comforting her, but there was only a kindly professional mask. She swung away to the window, trying to sort out her impressions. He still gave no sign of remembering her, and she was glad of it. Only Hetta mattered. She took a deep breath and turned back. She had her ghosts under control now, and they wouldn't be allowed to threaten the future.

A nurse looked in and handed Andrew some papers. They must be the test results, Elinor thought, her heart almost stopping with fear. He studied them, gave a grunt, then looked up.

'Splendid!' he said. 'Now we can get on.'

'You mean—'

'The heart's in excellent condition, and all Hetta's test results are good. We're cleared for take-off.'

She gave a gasp, pressing her hands over her mouth to fight back the sob of relief, and turned away. Her chest was heaving silently and she kept her back to him until she had herself under control. When she looked around he was gone.

CHAPTER FIVE

THE nurse gave Elinor a kindly smile. 'I know,' she said. 'Good news can be just as shattering as bad. Now I'll take you to her.'

Hetta was waiting on a trolley. She smiled and held out her arms to Elinor, and they hugged each other.

'It's really it, this time,' she said.

'Yes, this time.'

'Geronimo!'

'Geronimo!'

Elinor tried to sound strong but the word must have come out wonkier than she meant, because Hetta gave a small frown of concern.

'It's all right, Mummy.' Her voice became severe. 'Stop worrying.'

'Who's worrying?'

'You are. You always fret about things, and it's going to be all right.'

'Of course it is,' Elinor said firmly.

'Of course it is,' said a voice over her head.

Andrew was standing there, still in his dinner jacket, looking as cheerful and unconcerned as a man about to embark on a social evening. 'I'm Andrew,' he told Hetta, holding out his hand to her. 'We met once before.'

'Oh, yes. You looked different then.' She shook his hand, eyeing his expensive dinner jacket. 'You weren't prettied up like now.'

One of the nurses grunted with laughter, but it died under his gaze.

'Did I take you away from something nice?' Hetta asked, like a polite little old lady.

'No, something very boring that I was glad to get out of. It wasn't as important as you.'

'Will my op take very long?'

'It'll be as fast as I can make it, but you won't know anything. It's a doddle, you know. I do them all the time. Now, are you all ready?'

'Yes, thank you.'

Hetta smiled, and the look she gave him was full of trust and confidence.

It's the sedation, Elinor thought. *It's relaxing her already.*

But she knew it was more than that. A transformation had come over Andrew. His stiffness had fallen away, leaving behind a friendly, informal man, with nothing to do but make a little girl feel happy.

'Who's this?' he asked, indicating the furry bear. 'A friend of yours?'

'He's Samson. We've always been together.'

'Then he's a very important bear, and he should stay with you,' Andrew said solemnly, tucking the sheet about the two of them as he spoke. 'Keep him safe.'

Hetta giggled, and Elinor sent silent thanks to Andrew for what he was doing. However all this had come about, Hetta was in the right hands.

The nurses were beginning to wheel the trolley away. Elinor followed, her hand clasped in her child's. There was so much she wanted to say, but Hetta's eyelids were already drooping. All too soon they reached the doors through which Hetta must go and she could not, to a place from which she might never return.

'Love you, darling.'

'Love you, Mummy. Night, night.'

The doors opened, the corridor swallowed her up. She was gone. Suddenly Elinor was full of fear. She had longed for this moment, and now it was here she faced the reality she'd avoided before. She might never see Hetta alive again. This was make or break.

'Oh, God!' she whispered. 'Hetta—*Hetta*—'

'You've done everything for her that you can,' Andrew said. He'd been walking behind them. 'Now you have to trust someone else.'

'I do, I do trust you,' she said swiftly. 'But she's my baby, it's been just the two of us all her life.'

'What about her father?'

'I divorced Tom Landers soon after she was born and I haven't seen him since. Nor do I want to. It's just Hetta and me. If she dies, there's nothing left for me—nothing, nothing! No hope, or happiness, or anything to believe in. Without her, there's no reason to go on.'

As if in a dream he said, 'And yet it is possible to survive terrible grief. Even if all happiness has died, you can find a way to go on.'

There was a strange note in his voice that told her the words were wrenched from the depths of his own heart. Her head jerked up. Looking straight into his eyes, she saw there everything he'd tried to deny. He'd known her from the first moment. Of course he had.

He strove to recover, engulfing her hands in his strong ones. 'Trust me,' he said firmly. 'I will always do everything I can for her—and for you.'

Abruptly he dropped her hands and stepped back. 'I'll go and get scrubbed up. My assistant does the first part, and they'll need me in about half an hour.' He met her eyes again. 'I'll bring her back to you. I promise.'

He walked away without another word. Elinor watched him go, pressing her hands to her mouth, biting back the words she wanted to cry out.

Don't remember that you offered me the best of yourself, and I threw it back at you. Don't remember that I murdered all happiness for you. I didn't know that until this moment.

She pulled herself together. That was years ago. They were different people, and Andrew hadn't reacted to her because their past was unimportant to him. And that was right, because only Hetta mattered now.

Hours passed. Elinor was oblivious to them although she later learned the operation had taken two and a half hours. But minutes were different. She felt every second of every endless minute.

Outside the windows the darkness began to turn to grey as the night passed. She didn't see it, nor the opening of the door. She'd gone too far into another world where there was only suffering and hope, and was aware of nothing until a cup of tea appeared on the low table before her, and Andrew sat down in a nearby chair. He was still in his operating clothes.

'All done,' he said briefly. 'It went like a dream. She should make a complete recovery.'

'Really? Honestly?'

'I wouldn't say so if it wasn't true.'

Elinor buried her face in her hands and sat shaking in silence. He sipped his tea, pretending not to notice.

'Can I go to her?' she asked, raising her head at last.

'In a minute. They're taking her into Intensive Care, and you can go there and be with her when she comes round.'

'Did you really let her keep that smelly old toy all the time?'

He shook his head. 'It wouldn't be practical. But I never distress a child by saying so. I tell them what they want to hear, take the toy away when they've gone under, then make sure it's with them when they wake up. It's a deception, but it makes them happy and, I believe, helps them pull through.'

'You must have a gift for children.'

He shrugged. 'Not really. It's just a trick Elmer taught me. Drink your tea, and then I'll take you to her. Have you got strong nerves?' He shot out the question abruptly.

'What do you mean?'

'You'll be shocked by the sight. She's attached to a dozen machines and they look terrifying, but they're there to help her. When she wakes up don't let her see you're upset. Bursting into tears is the worst possible thing for her.'

'I don't burst into tears,' Elinor said quietly. 'I did when she first became ill. Not any more.'

'Of course. I shouldn't have said that to you,' he said wearily. 'I'm sorry.'

She wanted to say that he had nothing to be sorry for, but he'd already risen and was walking away, calling, 'Come along,' over his shoulder.

A young nurse admitted them to the intensive care

unit and led them to a bed in the far corner. Despite her brave words Elinor experienced a reaction when she saw Hetta, lying still, attached to what seemed like a dozen machines. For a moment she couldn't move while she fought back the tears.

'Steady,' Andrew said quietly beside her. 'Take a deep breath.'

'I'm all right,' she said at last. 'It's just—her colour—' Hetta was a cross between yellow and grey.

'Everyone is that colour at this stage,' Andrew said. 'I know it looks bad, but it's not worrying. Come over and let me explain the machines, then they won't seem so bad. These monitor her heartbeat, her blood pressure, the amount of painkiller she's being given. This one is feeding her through a drip, this one is giving her a blood transfusion.'

'That pipe fixed in her mouth—?'

'It goes to this machine here that's doing her breathing for her. Soon she'll be ready to come off it and take control of her own breathing.'

He went on talking, and Elinor lost track of the individual words. What continued to reach her was the quiet kindliness of his voice, calming her fears, offering her the equivalent of a steadying hand.

But suddenly his voice grew sharper as he demanded, 'Where's Samson?'

'Who?' The young nurse was staring as if he'd gone crazy.

'Samson. He's a toy bear. He must be here when she wakes up. Call the operating theatre. Find out what they did with him.' He was rapping out commands now.

The nurse made the call and elicited the information that Samson had been put aside and gone missing.

'Tell them to find him or heads will roll,' Andrew snapped.

'But, sir—'

'I promised that child, and if the promise is broken it could impede her recovery. I don't intend that to happen. Understood?'

The nurse threw him an alarmed look and turned back to the phone.

'Don't worry,' Andrew told Elinor. 'This will get sorted.'

Samson arrived a few minutes later, much the worse for wear, having fallen on the floor and been kicked into a corner by the busy operating staff. Andrew eyed him, recognising the impossibility of putting this filthy object into Hetta's arms.

'Nurse, have you got some disinfectant soap?' he asked. 'Strong.'

'Yes, sir.'

'Get it, please.'

The nurse hurried back with the soap, but was immediately summoned to another bed. Her face said the washing of toys wasn't part of her job on such a high-tension ward.

'I'll do it,' Elinor said.

'There's a wash basin attached to the wall over there,' Andrew said. 'You can keep Hetta in your sights all the time.'

She hurried across and got to work on Samson, who rapidly became his original bright yellow colour. Even his daft smile seemed to have brightened. As she worked Elinor sometimes glanced over to Hetta, where Andrew was still checking the machines. He seemed satisfied, she noted with relief. Then he looked up, saw her watching, gave a brief nod and strode off.

Elinor crept back to Hetta's side, clutching the damp toy. One of the nurses produced a chair for her. Then there was a light touch on her shoulder. It was another nurse, holding something out to her.

'It belongs to Mr Blake's secretary,' she said. 'She keeps it in the office. He said to lend it to you.'

It was a hair-dryer. He'd even thought of that.

Elinor turned the dryer onto Samson until he was bone-dry, then slipped him gently under Hetta's hand. At once the little fingers flexed and tightened around him, although she gave no other sign of life.

Time ticked past. Hetta lay motionless, tiny, seemingly fixed like this for ever.

Andrew arrived again and spoke to the nurse. 'Let's see if she can breathe by herself. Would you mind standing back, please?' This to Elinor.

She got out of their way and watched tensely as the great tube was untied and drawn out of Hetta's mouth. There was a moment when the world seemed to stand still, then her chest heaved and she gave a big sigh.

'Excellent,' Andrew said. 'Couldn't be better. Mrs Landers, you should go and have some breakfast.'

'How can I leave her?'

'She's passed the first milestone successfully, and you'll do better by her if you keep your own strength up. There's an all-night canteen on the top floor. Go and eat. I don't want you fainting under my feet.'

Having barked at her, he strode out, leaving her with only an impression of how exhausted he'd looked after being up all night, and the day was only just starting.

She didn't know if he managed to grab a nap somewhere, but he looked in at about four-hour intervals after that, and was there when Hetta finally opened her eyes.

''Lo, Mummy.'

'Hallo, darling.' But Hetta's eyes had already closed again. 'Darling,' she repeated urgently.

'Leave her,' Andrew said. 'That's as good as you can hope for now.'

He left. After another hour Hetta stirred again. This time she looked at her mother, smiled and fell back to sleep. The day wore on. It was late afternoon before Hetta awoke properly.

''Lo, Mummy,' she said again, but this time she sounded brighter.

Elinor slipped to the floor so that her face should be closer to Hetta's.

'Darling, welcome back.'

'Have I been away?'

'Yes, but you're back now, thank God.'

Hetta looked around her anxiously. 'Where's Samson?'

'He's here,' Elinor said, lifting him to within her view. 'You were cuddling him.'

'But that's not Samson,' Hetta protested.

'It is, darling.'

'It isn't, it isn't.' Hetta was becoming distressed. A nurse anxiously tried to soothe her, but tears began to roll down Hetta's face. Elinor's attempts to reassure her only made the child cry bitterly. This was the worst possible thing for her wounded chest, and Elinor looked around wildly, desperate for help.

'Hey, what's all this?' Andrew said, appearing out of the blue, it seemed to Elinor.

'I want Samson,' Hetta wept. 'You promised.'

'And I always keep my promises,' Andrew said, lounging by her bed, apparently at ease, although his skin was the colour of parchment and there were black shadows under his eyes. 'Samson's been with you all the time—well, almost all. You see, while we were making you as good as new, we thought we'd do the same for him. So we tidied him up and gave him a bath, which he badly needed.'

Hetta's eyes were on him, and she'd stopped crying. 'He doesn't like being bathed,' she said.

'So I gather. His language was frightful. It made the nurses blush.'

Hetta giggled.

'But it's still Samson,' Andrew said. 'You can see by that little tear in his ear.'

'That was Daisy's cat,' Hetta whispered.

'Uh-huh! I gather it was quite a fight. So you see, it's Samson all right, so why don't you just tuck him up against you—like that—and—?'

Hetta was already asleep.

'That's wonderful,' Elinor said. 'How did you ever—?'

'One moment, please, Mrs Landers. Nurse—'

He became deep in discussion with the nurse for several minutes, and when he'd finished the moment had passed. Elinor had turned back to Hetta, watching her with loving, obsessive eyes, and Andrew slipped away quietly without disturbing her.

For the first week Elinor barely left Hetta. When she needed sleep there was a side room with basic beds, where she would snatch a nap before hurrying back.

At first she watched her with incredulous delight, hardly able to believe that this delicate little creature had survived such a massive onslaught.

Yet Hetta's frailty was increasingly an illusion. For the first time in two years she had a strong heart, working normally. For days she was woozy and sometimes confused from the massive anaesthetic, but the signs of improvement were coming fast, and already her colour was better.

'She's our star patient,' said the nurse in Intensive Care. 'She took over her own breathing at the first possible moment, and since then she's done everything right on time.'

And Elinor was feeling cheerful enough to smile and say, 'I'll swear it's the first time in her life she's done what anyone wanted without argument.'

Hetta giggled. 'I'm a devil, aren't I, Mummy?'

'I thought you were asleep, you cheeky little madam.'

As she came off the machines she was moved into a larger ward, where there were other children, and promptly brightened life with a feud with a little boy in the next bed. Elinor began returning to the boarding house to sleep. Gradually she found she could leave Hetta without worrying if she would still be alive on her return.

Best of all, Hetta's wicked sense of humour had returned, and she liked nothing so much as to tease her mother. The long wound in her chest, so terrifying to Elinor, filled the child with ghoulish pride.

'Isn't it great?' she demanded when the dressing

had been removed and Andrew was examining the dark red line.

'If you like that kind of thing,' Elinor said faintly.

'But we do, don't we?' Andrew said to Hetta.

'Yes, we do,' Hetta said firmly. 'Honestly, Mummy, it was a great big electric saw—'

'*What?*'

'That's how we get through the breastbone to find the heart,' Andrew explained. 'You can't do this operation by playing peek-a-boo through the ribs.'

Hetta giggled and she and Andrew exchanged the glances of conspirators. It wasn't lost on Elinor that the nurse, standing deferentially behind him, was staring at him with astonishment.

As he walked out she followed him quickly. 'What do you mean by talking like that with a child?' she demanded.

'She loves it. It's adults who are squeamish, not children.' The friendly ease he'd shown the child was gone, and he was tense again. 'Good day, Mrs Landers.'

Elinor had to admit that he was right. Hetta was having the time of her life. In no time she'd become the leader of the children's ward, in the heart of any anarchy that was going. To Elinor it was a joy to see her being occasionally naughty. It was so long since she'd had the energy.

Between her and Andrew there had developed a perfect understanding, and she called him Andrew, with his encouragement. To the little girl he wasn't the figure of awe he presented to his staff. He was the friend who'd understood about Samson, and would understand anything she said to him. So to him she confided her nightmares. He listened, nodding in perfect comprehension. Elinor came upon them one day in time to hear him say, 'Do the rocks ever actually fall on you, or does it just look as if they might?'

'I keep thinking they're going to, but I wake up first.'

'Well, it's only the anaesthetic—you know that, don't you?'

'After all this time?'

'Do you know how much we had to give you to knock you out for a process as big as this?'

'How much?' she demanded, fascinated.

He made a wide gesture with his hands. '*This* much.'

'Wow!'

'So you don't get rid of it all at once. It works its way out gradually, and it gives you funny thoughts and dreams. But that's all it is. So the next time you see those rocks, just tell them you're not scared of them, because they're not real.'

Hetta nodded, reassured.

'Why didn't she tell me she's having nightmares?' Elinor demanded of Andrew outside the ward.

'Because she knows you've been through a lot and she's protecting you from any more.'

'She told you that?'

'She didn't have to. Don't you realise that she's looking after you as much as you're looking after her? She's very like you in many ways.'

Then something seemed to occur to him, and he bid her goodnight. He often did that when their paths crossed, and it saddened her.

After the day of the operation, when they'd made contact, she'd somehow believed that soon they would talk about the past, and how they had met again. Perhaps she would have a chance to tell him that she was sorry, and ask his forgiveness. But as the days until Hetta was discharged from hospital narrowed down to four, then three, she realised that it wasn't going to happen.

And after all, she mused, why should it? Their paths had crossed by accident, and doubtless he would be glad to see the back of her. She probably embarrassed him.

But she would always be grateful to him. Theirs had been a sad, stormy relationship that had ended in anger, but now they'd been given a postscript that softened the bitterness.

She doubted that his bitterness had lasted very long. She knew he'd made a success of his life, just as he'd always vowed. She pictured him married to a brilliant society woman, someone whose sophistication could match his own. How glad he must be to have escaped herself.

As for her, why should she be bitter? It was she who had injured him, and if she'd paid for it with years of disappointment and disaster, perhaps that was only justice.

Elinor's money was running dangerously low, and she started working again, accepting freelance beauty assignments that didn't take her too far away. She had just completed a lucrative job and was feeling cheerful as she headed for the hospital in the early evening. This was Hetta's last night, and tomorrow she would be coming home to the boarding house.

She found Hetta in high spirits, competing with the

boy opposite to see who could put their tongue out furthest.

'I should think they'll be glad to see the back of you tomorrow,' she said comically, sitting on Hetta's bed.

Hetta nodded, accepting this as a compliment, and they laughed together.

'Are you all ready to go?'

Hetta nodded vigorously. 'Home!' she carolled. 'I'm going home.'

A sound made Elinor glance up quickly, smiling when she saw Daisy. But the smile faded at the look on her friend's face. Daisy seemed distracted with worry, and she beckoned Elinor urgently into the corridor.

'I'm sorry to land this on you, on top of everything else, luv.'

'Daisy, whatever's happened?'

'That Mr Jenson in number six,' Daisy said with loathing. 'Stayed in bed this morning, with a cold, he said. But he took his smokes with him and fell asleep. We were all lucky to get out alive.'

'You mean—?'

'A terrible fire we had, soon after you left this morning. Top floor burned out. Everything black with smoke. And now the fire service say the building's unsafe. They let us back for a few minutes to get our things, but that's all. I brought your stuff.'

For the first time Elinor noticed her suitcases on the floor, and she began to feel sick as the full implications of this reached her. Daisy read her expression without trouble.

'The insurance will cover it,' she said, 'but in the meantime nobody can live there. The two students have gone to a hostel, Mr Jenson has dumped himself on his sister and she's welcome to him. I've found a little hotel nearby, where I can keep an eye on the rebuilding. But I don't know what you'll do.'

'It's all right,' Elinor said, trying to sound calm. 'We'll find somewhere. You've been wonderful to us, Daisy. Now you've got to think of yourself.'

She maintained a cheerful front until she was alone, but then the shock of her situation came over her. In a few hours Hetta would be discharged, and she had nowhere to take her. Daisy's place had been shabby, but it had also been clean and comfortable. There she could have tended Hetta in peace, with Daisy's kindly help. Now she was alone in a cold desert.

She pulled herself together. Whatever happened Hetta must never suspect anything was wrong. She was smiling as she returned to her child, and sat with her, making their own silly little jokes until Hetta fell asleep.

As darkness fell the night shift began to appear. The nurse in charge swept her eyes over the patients, and frowned at the sight of Elinor, sitting in a chair, her suitcases hidden unconvincingly under the bed. Elinor's nervousness grew. Nurse Stewart was a well-meaning woman, and not deliberately unkind. But her mind was rigid. To her there was only one 'right' way of doing things, and that was the way prescribed by the rules. She was also a busybody, happiest when imposing her views on others.

'Mrs Landers,' she said, 'a moment, if you please.'

She swept on to her desk, and Elinor followed her reluctantly.

'Visiting time is over, you know,' Nurse Stewart said. 'I really must ask you to leave.'

'But I can't,' Elinor said desperately. 'I've nowhere to go. The place I lived burned down today. I've only just heard.'

'Is that why you have your suitcases with you?'

'Yes. Someone rescued my things.'

'I see. Well, that's very unfortunate, of course,' the nurse said in the tone she would have used to describe a shortfall of bandages, 'but this is not a hotel. There are no provisions in the rules for overnight accommodation.'

'But I was allowed to stay just after the operation.'

'Ah, yes, when your little girl was in danger, and in the intensive care unit, but she's on a general ward now, and the danger is long over. In fact, I believe she's due to be discharged tomorrow.'

'But where?' Elinor said desperately. 'I've nowhere to take her now.'

'You'd better start looking for somewhere else first thing.'

Somewhere else meant a place that would demand a deposit, and the money she'd made recently wouldn't run to that. Elinor's despair must have shown in her eyes for the nurse, with a plain attempt to be helpful, said, 'I'm sure the social services will help you. There are homes for children with special needs. I'll find you the number.'

'No,' Elinor choked. 'I don't want anyone taking her over. I want her with me.'

'But I'm sure you realise that Hetta's best interests must come first.'

'Her best interests mean a proper home with her mother.'

'But you don't have one, do you?' Nurse Stewart said, smiling blandly.

To Elinor that smile was horrible. It was the face of the pitiless world that had done its best to crush her, and would keep trying until her strength was exhausted. She felt some frightening, uncontrollable feeling rising in her. If it reached the surface it would emerge as screams, she knew it.

Turning, she ran out of the ward, along the corridor and down the stairs until she reached the ground, then out into the hospital garden. Terror and panic were mounting in her as she ran and ran, until at last she collided with a tree and stayed just as she was, clutching the trunk and giving way to her grief.

She'd fought and fought, and given it everything she had. But it wasn't enough, and suddenly she had no more strength to fight.

CHAPTER SIX

ELINOR had held onto her control through everything, refusing to let herself weep no matter how bad things had become. But now it all caught up with her like a wave that had been growing from a great distance until it crashed over her without mercy, leaving her shaking and helpless in the grip of sobs.

'*No!*' she screamed. 'Not any more, please. There has to be an end somewhere. *No more—no—please—*'

'Is something wrong?' asked a man's voice behind her.

'Go away,' she cried passionately. 'Yes, something's wrong. Everything's wrong and there's nobody to help. *Go away!*'

She heard a step, as though someone had moved closer, and Andrew said, 'There *is* someone to help.'

She swung around, tears pouring down her face. She was beyond speech, beyond dismay that he'd found her like this, beyond hope or fear. She could do nothing but lean against the tree in helpless, shuddering despair.

'I don't know what to do,' she said huskily. 'There's always one more thing and I'm falling apart. I mustn't—for Hetta's sake—but I am, I am, and there's nowhere to go—oh, God!—'

She wept freely, not even trying to cover her face. Her strength had collapsed all in a moment and there was nothing left.

Andrew took hold of her shoulders gently. 'Has something happened to Hetta?' he asked. 'Do you want me to go to her?'

'No, she's fine,' Elinor choked.

'If she's fine, everything's fine. Ellie, do you hear that? If Hetta is safe and well, nothing else matters. Cling to it. Any other problem can be solved.'

But she could barely hear him. Anguish shook her, wrung her out, drained her. He was so close to her that she could feel his breath, and put up her hands as if to fend him off, shaking her head from side to side.

'No,' she gasped, 'no, it's no use—don't you understand? Nothing's any use because as fast as you cope with one thing—there's always something else—it's like—there's someone up there who's going to throw one thing after another into my path until I give in—and—and—'

'OK, OK,' he said. 'You're having hysterics, and it's no wonder after what you've been through, but it's going to be fine—'

'What do you know?' she demanded, not screaming but speaking in a low, hoarse whisper. 'There's nothing you or anyone can do about this. They're going to take her away from me and I can't stop them.'

All her control had gone and grief poured out of her in ugly hee-hawing sobs. Andrew wasted no more time in talking but put his arms about her and pulled her hard against his chest.

'All right,' he murmured. 'Let it come. You've fought it long enough, don't try any more.'

'I can't cope with anything else,' she sobbed.

'There's no need to. You're not alone.'

'Yes, I am, I've always been alone. Oh, you don't have to tell me it's my own fault—'

'I wasn't going to—'

'I know it, and I can survive if it's just me, but it's not fair on Hetta, she's never had any kind of life—'

'But she's going to have a great life now,' he said, trying to be heard through her torrent of words.

'She should have had a better mother, someone who knew what to do and didn't go blundering through life making mistakes and getting it all wrong, and, oh, God! *Oh, God!*'

He gave up trying to get through to her and held her tightly while the storm raged. When he finally felt her calm down a little he put his hands either side of her face.

'Listen to me,' he said severely. 'Whatever it is, something can be done, *yes, it can,*' he added quickly as she tried to speak. 'This is just nerves because you've been through so much and it's all caught up with you in one go. But it's not like you to give in.'

'You don't know what's like me,' she whispered.

'I know you always had a lot of courage.'

'Not really. Way back then—I was all talk. I didn't know what life was about.'

'And you think you know now?'

'It's about betrayal,' she said quietly, 'and fighting, and things always turning out wrong, and knowing it was your own fault because you're stupid.'

'You're not stupid. Don't talk about yourself like that. Now tell me what brought this on. Why should Hetta be taken away from you?'

'Because I've nowhere for us to live. The guest house where we've been staying burned down today and she's due out of here tomorrow.'

'Then we'll find somewhere else for you to go.'

'How can I? I've no money and Nurse Stewart wants to bring in social services, and they'll take her away from me—'

'Of course they won't,' he said firmly. 'They're not ogres. They know Hetta needs her mother. As for Stewart, what on earth made you confide in that stupid woman?'

'I couldn't help it. She found me—I'm not supposed to be here at night—'

'But you've nowhere else. Right. Leave her to me.'

He relaxed his grip, giving her space to draw back and see his face. In the dark it was hard to make out details, but she could see that it was hard and set, and radiated confidence. Even so, 'You won't make Nurse Stewart back down,' she said.

He raised his eyebrows. 'I'm commonly held to have a little authority around here. Even over her. Come on.'

He took her elbow and led her back through the trees. As they approached the lights of the building he released her and said firmly, 'Keep quiet and leave everything to me.'

'All right.' Her fear had gone. The total confidence and authority of this man was beyond question. He could do anything.

His manner as he entered the ward was impeccably formal, and Nurse Stewart hurried forward, eyeing Elinor suspiciously.

'A very serious problem has developed,' she hurried to say. 'Hetta Landers is suddenly homeless, and I really feel it's my duty to—'

'To inform me,' Andrew interrupted her smoothly.

'You were quite right, but Mrs Landers has already consulted me, and I have the problem in hand.'

'I'm sure you agree that it's a matter for the proper authorities. A vulnerable child must not be—'

'Must not be parted from her mother,' Andrew interrupted again, and this time in a manner that made it plain he was taking charge of the conversation. 'I have a good friend who's highly placed in the social services. I've already contacted him, and there's no need for you to take any action.'

Nurse Stewart's mouth tightened, and Elinor guessed that to be told to do nothing was ashes to her.

'Of course, if you have the matter in hand...' she said reluctantly. 'May I know the name of this friend?'

There was a silence, during which Andrew's face assumed the frozen, stony look that his staff dreaded. Elinor thought she would die if he ever turned that look on her. And then she remembered the night that he had.

'Are you implying that you do not believe me, Nurse?' Andrew asked very, very quietly.

Even Nurse Stewart blenched at his tone, but she rallied. 'Certainly not, but if he should be in touch—'

'It will be with me, not you. Now, Mrs Landers, if you'll collect your things, I'm sure your friends will be here for you soon.'

Dazed, Elinor drew her cases quietly from under the bed, managing not to disturb Hetta. Andrew took one from her and strode out of the ward, with her following.

Not a word was uttered while they went along the corridor and into a lift. But when the doors were safely shut and they were on their way down Elinor ventured to say, 'Suppose she checks up to find out if you told the truth?'

He turned astonished eyes on her. 'Check up? On me?'

There it was again, that total dominating authority that expected no challenge. It wasn't even arrogant. It didn't need to be.

'But all those things you said—what will she do when nothing happens?'

He regarded her with faint amusement. 'But something *will* happen. I'm going to make it happen.' His mouth assumed a sardonic twist. 'Don't you think I can?'

'Oh, yes,' she said, meaning it. 'I think you could do just about anything.'

Two floors down they left the lift and headed along another corridor, and a door.

'This is my office. You can stay here tonight. There's a small bathroom through there, so you won't need to go out for any reason. Stretch out on the sofa, keep the door locked and don't answer to anyone except me. I'll be here at five-thirty in the morning. That way, I'll be ahead of the cleaner, who comes at six. Here's a small travelling alarm. Set it for five o'clock. Have I forgotten anything?'

'I can't imagine you forgetting anything. Thank you so much. I just don't know how to—'

'No need,' he said quickly. 'Goodnight.'

He vanished fast, leaving her regarding the closed door. Slowly she locked it, feeling dizzy after the events of that evening. But as she settled herself on the sofa and turned out the light she felt a strange calm descend on her. On the surface things were no better. She still had nowhere to take Hetta next day. But Andrew had said he would take care of it. And that made her feel safe.

Now she could relax enough to fall asleep. As her consciousness blurred she felt she were back again in the garden, racked with torment, pouring out her heart to him, feeling the comfort of his arms about her.

That shouldn't have happened, she thought. It had reminded her of things best forgotten. For years she'd hidden away the memory of what it had felt like to be held by him. Two husbands had come and gone, both of them bad mistakes. She'd survived by not comparing them to the man whose love she'd thrown away because she'd been too young and stupid to appreciate it.

She'd learned its value when it had been too late, and then she'd buried him deep in the dark places of her mind. It had been that or go mad with regret.

Now an ironic accident had forced her to remember. In the darkness it was as though he were there with her again, warming her, murmuring in her ear, just as once he'd whispered words of love and touched her face with his lips.

It was unendurable. She went into the bathroom, stripped off and got under the shower, trying to wash away all the weariness and desperation of her life. But as she stepped out she passed a long mirror, and what she saw gave her a shock. As a professional beautician Elinor knew how to make the best of herself so that her customers would trust her, and with the excellent cosmetics always within her reach she never looked less than well groomed.

But now, gazing back at her was the truth, and she saw, without defences, what the years had done to her. The last time she'd been in his arms her body had been young, rounded, bursting with life. Now she was too thin, her face drawn, her eyes haunted. The glorious mane of blonde hair that he'd loved and through which he'd run his fingers had long gone, hacked off in bitterness some time in her dreadful second marriage. Now it was short and neat, easy to care for, and that was all.

This haunted, desperate woman was what he'd held against him tonight. If he'd thought at all about the beauty he'd once loved it would be with disgust that it had so faded.

It was only then that she remembered that tonight he'd called her Ellie.

Andrew was there on the dot of five-thirty next morning, knocking softly. Elinor was already up, and she let him in. He'd brought her a cup of tea in a paper cup, which she drank down thankfully.

'Any disturbances?' he asked.

'Not one.'

'Good. Now, here's what's going to happen.'

As he spoke he paced the floor, somehow never looking at her.

'Last night I called a friend of mine, who's about to rush off on a business trip, and doesn't want to leave his house empty. The person who was going to look after it for him has let him down at the last moment, and he would be delighted if you'd take over. It's about ten miles from the hospital, on the edge of the country. And the pay is good, so you wouldn't have to leave Hetta in order to work.'

'Pay? You mean he'd actually pay me when he's

giving me accommodation?' she asked, hardly daring to believe this.

'There'd be some work. You'd keep the house clean—although most of it is shut up—keep it warm, make sure everyone knew it wasn't empty.'

'And I could forward his mail,' she said quickly.

That made him turn to her, and a strange look passed over his face, as though he was completely taken aback.

'Yes,' he said vaguely, 'although I don't think there would be much. He has it redirected.'

'But I could answer the telephone, and tell people where he is,' she offered, anxious to do more than the light duties prescribed.

'You could do that,' he agreed, but in the same strange fashion, as though he was thinking of something else. 'So I can tell my friend that you agree?'

'I'd be glad to. But he doesn't know anything about me.'

'He'll accept my recommendation.'

'Can I call him, to say thank you?'

'I'll get him to call you when you're there.'

'What's his name?'

'I think you should go now. You must need food. Go up to the all night canteen, and I'll see you later.'

The canteen was serving an early breakfast. Elinor discovered that she was ravenous, and piled her plate with eggs and bacon. At this hour the place was filled with doctors and nurses, weary-eyed after night duty, or just snatching a mouthful before starting their day. Among them she was dismayed to recognise Nurse Stewart.

The older woman's eyes were like gimlets, and Elinor guessed she was furious at being denied the

chance to interfere. She'd had to yield before
Andrew's authority, but she was unforgiving. She
headed straight for Elinor's table and sat down without asking.

'You're here early, Mrs Landers. May I ask where
you spent the night?'

'You may not,' Elinor said angrily. 'You have no
more say about my daughter, since I gather your shift
has finished. As soon as possible I'll be going to the
ward to prepare her to come home.'

'But which home? That *is* a question I may legit-
imately ask?'

'Good morning, ladies,' came a voice from above
their heads, and they both looked up to see Andrew
about to sit down with them. 'Mrs Landers, I'm delighted to find you here. I telephoned Mr Martin, and
he's delighted with his new housekeeper. The place
is ready for your immediate occupation, and if you
contact my secretary later this morning she'll give
you full details.

'There'll also be a chart explaining Hetta's medication, to prevent her body rejecting her new heart,
but I understand you already know a lot about that.
The nurses say you always watch carefully when she
has her pills. Well done. The district nurse is being
informed about your arrival, and will call every day.
But I don't expect any problems. Nurse Stewart, how
nice to see you again. I hope you're eating well. You
need to keep your strength up after a night shift. I
always say night work is the most exhausting, because your blood sugar's low. Have you found that,
or do you manage to...'

He talked on, barely stopping for breath, giving the
nurse no time to raise problems. Watching him with

admiration, Elinor realised that this was a consummate performance, done for a purpose. Her instincts told her that this apparently outgoing man wasn't the Andrew she knew, either years ago or now. He was forcing himself, and although his manner was light his intent was deadly serious.

But there was a stubborn look in Nurse Stewart's eyes that said she wouldn't be beaten. However long Andrew stayed, she could stay longer, to poke and probe at Elinor's defences, in order, ultimately, to impose her own 'right' solution. And when Andrew's pager went it seemed that the nurse had won.

'Apparently I'm wanted,' Andrew said. 'Mrs Landers, may I trouble you to come with me? There are some final matters to discuss. Good morning, Nurse Stewart. It was a pleasure talking to you.'

His hand was under her elbow, guiding her into the corridor, and then he was breathing out like a schoolboy who'd successfully brought off a prank.

'Thank heavens you came!' she said.

'I only thought of the danger when you'd gone. Did I get there in time to avoid disaster?'

'By a whisker.'

'You'd best get out of here to a place where she can't follow.'

'Is there such a place?'

'Here's the keys to my car. This is the registration number.' He scribbled it for her. 'Get in the back, pull the rug over you and finish your night's sleep. See my secretary in four hours, and give her the keys.'

'Is that safe?' Elinor asked.

'Completely. She's the most discreet woman in the world.'

His car was brand-new and the very last word in luxury and success. There was room to lie down in comfort in the back seat, and pull the mohair rug over her head so that the outside world couldn't see her. Like this she felt warm and protected.

Protected.

Andrew's doing.

On the dot of ten Elinor presented herself to Andrew's secretary, who received the keys without comment and gave her a letter from him that she'd just finished typing.

It began 'Dear Mrs Landers' and informed her, politely and formally, that all arrangements were in place and a cab had been arranged to take her to the house. Mr Martin understood about Hetta and she would arrive to find the place already warm. Her salary would be paid directly into her bank, if she would kindly give the details to his secretary. A set of keys was enclosed, he wished her well, etc. etc.

Going to the ward, she found the day staff there, under the charge of Nurse Edwards, a cheerful figure whom Hetta liked.

'All ready to go?' she said, smiling. 'I gather you're going to be a housekeeper at a nice place on the edge of town.'

'Aren't we going back to Daisy's?' Hetta asked.

'No, darling. They had a fire yesterday.'

'Mr Jenson,' Hetta said at once, in her wise old lady voice. 'Smoking in bed again. Poor Daisy. What will she do?'

'She's got a room nearby, and the insurance will take care of the rebuilding,' Elinor explained. 'And we're going to look after this man's house for him.'

'Why don't you let the nurse finish dressing Hetta
while I give you her medication?' Nurse Edwards
suggested.

It was like a dream to be getting ready to leave.
Only a short time ago her skies had been dark. Now
she had hope again, and it was thanks to one person.

'I think I'd better find Andrew and say thank you,'
Elinor said.

'I've said my "thank yous",' Hetta explained. 'He
came earlier. He said he was sorry he couldn't see
you, but he was operating this morning, and would
be busy all day.'

So that was that. He'd taken every chance to ensure
he didn't meet her again before she left. And perhaps,
on the whole, it was best.

As promised, the cab was waiting for her, and in a
few minutes they were gliding away from the hospital. Then the suburbs began to fall away and they
were in the country. The houses grew further apart,
more luxurious, and she realised that she was in a
moneyed district, where the buildings weren't houses
at all, but 'residences', with drives, and wrought-iron
gates.

At last the car turned into a gate more decorative
than the others. She just had time to observe the sign
reading 'Oaks' before they began the journey up a
winding drive, thickly lined with trees. Then the trees
parted without warning, giving her a sudden view of
the mansion.

It was awesome. She'd expected a rich man's residence, but this had a style and luxury that trumpeted
a message to the world. No wonder Mr Martin, whoever he was, didn't care to leave the place empty.

The cab driver waited while she opened the front

door and carried her bags in for her, but waved away
her money.

'Already paid, ma'am,' he said. 'Including the tip.'

Then they were alone, looking around and around
in awe.

'Goodness, Mummy!' Hetta exclaimed. 'It's like a
film set.'

'It is, isn't it?'

'Is it real?'

'I don't think it can be.'

They explored together, first the kitchen, a blue and
white masterpiece of luxury and modern equipment.

'It's a bit over-the-top for egg and chips,' was
Hetta's down-to-earth comment. This was her favourite dish.

'I rather think it was designed for cordon bleu,'
Elinor mused.

'But you could do egg and chips?' Hetta asked anxiously.

'For an army, darling.'

The huge refrigerator was stocked to the roof: eggs,
rashers, sausages, vegetables, milk and six different
fruit juices. The freezer was likewise packed.

In stunned silence they climbed the broad curved
stairway to the realms above, where the corridor
branched into two corridors, each covered in thick
cream carpet. In one direction every door was locked,
but in the other they found two unlocked doors.
Opening the first they found a large corner bedroom,
with windows on two sides, and a modern four-poster
bed, hung with white lace.

'You could really be a film star in that,' Hetta
breathed.

They found her room opposite, also large, but more

down-to-earth. The bed was covered with a duvet depicting wildlife, which delighted Hetta. A study of the bookshelves produced more about wildlife, especially elephants, which pleased her even more. But even as she eagerly scanned the books Elinor saw her eyes begin to droop. She still had a long way to go before complete recovery, and the short journey had taken it out of her.

'Time for your nap, darling,' she said.

'Can I have something to eat first?'

Elinor dropped to one knee to look Hetta in the eyes. 'Of course you can,' she said. 'Of course you can,' she repeated, gathering the little girl against her in a passion of tenderness.

But Hetta was already nodding off in her arms. Elinor lifted her up.

'You can have anything you want,' she whispered, laying her on the bed and propping her up in a half-sitting position, as the hospital had advised until the wound in her chest had finished healing. 'Anything,' she repeated, pulling the duvet up to her chin, 'just as soon as you wake up.'

She slipped briefly downstairs to collect the bags, and unpacked them with her own and Hetta's doors open, in case the child should awaken and be alarmed at the strange surroundings. But she was deeply asleep. Even when Elinor dropped a heavy bag on the floor with a clatter Hetta did no more than sigh happily.

After watching her for a moment Elinor crept out and went on a tour of the house. As Andrew had explained, most of the doors were locked, which was a relief. Evidently her duties would be confined to their rooms upstairs, the kitchen, and the large living room equipped with satellite television and tuned into every conceivable station.

Hetta slept the afternoon away before awakening with an appetite. Elinor whipped her up an omelette and found some ice cream in the freezer. After that they spent a couple of contented hours exploring children's channels on the sofa, until Hetta dropped off again in her mother's arms.

This time, when she'd put her to bed, Elinor looked around the room and saw that here too was a small television with satellite channels. It was a child's room, as the decor made clear: a boy, she judged, from the cowboys on the wallpaper, and one who was denied nothing.

They had joked about film stars, but it wasn't a joke at all, really. The lace-hung four-poster was big enough to sleep six, and the private bathroom that led off from it was like a Hollywood fantasy, with a circular bath sunk into the floor, its elegant cream colour adorned by a jigsaw pattern all the way around the edge. All accessories were gold-plated, even—Elinor was amused to note—the toilet-roll holder. The soap dish held a new cake of cream soap, so heavily scented that she had to sit down after one sniff.

Before going to bed she tried the shower, and discovered that the water came out with real force and maintained its temperature. That was true luxury, she thought, drying off with one of the thick cream towels, and thinking of Daisy's shower attachment, which had to be tied onto the taps and always came off, no matter how tightly you fixed it.

She checked Hetta once more, before snuggling down blissfully in the soft white sheets of the big bed. She'd left both bedroom doors open again, with a light on in the hall between them, so that Hetta could be immediately reassured should she awaken. And in the middle of the night she heard the soft patter of feet and felt someone climb in beside her.

As they drifted off to sleep she wondered if she'd gone to heaven, for that was the only way to explain how her troubles had been swept away and replaced by this perfect peace and serenity. That was the stuff of fairy tales, not real life.

CHAPTER SEVEN

As ONE day slipped into the next nothing happened to disturb their peace. The district nurse called regularly to check Hetta's progress and confirm that she was doing well. She was a comfortable, motherly woman, and the other two were soon calling her Sally.

'Don't be worried if she still needs to sleep a lot,' she advised Elinor. 'She's been through the mill, and it'll be a long recovery. Take everything at her pace.'

Elinor had found a letter in the kitchen explaining the house's secrets to her, the use of each key, plus a set of keys that fitted a car in the garage that she could use. To her relief it was a modest family saloon rather than a luxurious vehicle that would have intimidated her. They began taking short trips to a nearby village where there were a few little shops. Elinor would buy a newspaper, and a few grocery items. They would have a snack in a small, rustic teashop, and then go home.

On one of these trips she tentatively put her cash card in the machine, fearing to find herself overdrawn. But the machine cheerfully reported a healthy balance. She stared. Obviously her first salary cheque had been paid in, but it seemed much larger than anything she'd expected.

She tried again, this time requesting a mini statement. Sure enough there had been a credit, which she regarded with disbelief. *That much?*

Obviously that was a month's money in advance, but even so.

What was Mr Martin? A philanthropist? Or just slightly crazy?

In a short time Hetta had become so much at ease that Elinor no longer needed to be there when she awoke from her nap. She would simply come downstairs and find her mother in the grounds where she often lingered to enjoy the summer weather.

The extent of those grounds meant that there was no chance to get acquainted with the neighbours, or even see them. Whoever they were, they existed in their own mansions, deep in their own grounds. Apart from Sally nobody came to the house, and they were completely self-contained. It was like existing in a separate world, where there was only quiet, and the chance to heal.

As the tensions drained away, she wondered when in her life before she'd known such total, spirit-healing peace. Not in her wretched marriage to Tom Landers. 'All teeth and trousers,' her mother had said angrily. 'You're a fool, girl. You've been a fool ever since you played fast and loose with the best man you ever knew, or ever will.'

And she'd laid a desperate hand over her mother's mouth because that had been a truth she hadn't been able to face, even on the eve of her wedding to Tom.

Before that, the short-lived marriage to Jack Smith. No peace there, only rows and bitterness, and a desperate attempt to cope with his drinking.

And before that...

She shut the thought off. She couldn't bear it now.

With the money now at her disposal Elinor was able to pay a few outstanding bills, plus the cost of a taxi to bring Daisy for a visit. There was a joyful reunion, Elinor persuaded her friend to stay the night, and when the taxi returned for her next morning she departed with the promise to return again soon.

There was no doubt that her visit had been good for Hetta, who was becoming bored as her strength increased. As she'd told Andrew, she longed for a dog. Failing that, a playmate of her own age. Elinor kept her amused as best she could and the two of them enjoyed the happiest times they'd ever known. But still, there were times when she knew Hetta needed more.

One morning while they were breakfasting and mulling over what to do with the day, there was a noise from the front hall, and she went out to find a letter on the mat, something that had never happened before. Mr Martin's mail was all redirected, but this one must have slipped through the net. She picked it up and was about to lay it on the hall table when the name caught her eye.

Andrew Blake.

It was a mistake, of course. Andrew and Mr Martin were friends. He'd simply asked if he could have some of his mail sent here.

But why? And in that case why didn't it say 'care of'? And why had Mr Martin never called her, as Andrew had said he would? Because there was no Mr Martin. This was Andrew's house. Of course it was. How could she have been so blind?

Or had she? Hadn't she at least suspected, and then turned her eyes away from the thought, not wanting to confront the implications?

All this time she'd been living here on his charity.

She hadn't known it, but he had known. Had he enjoyed the thought? Despised her? Laughed at her?

Could she blame him?

Now she could see how cleverly he'd arranged matters, redirecting his mail, having his calls diverted, locking so many rooms. He'd had to take a chance with the neighbours but even there he'd been lucky. They were too distant to pose any real problem.

The air around her head seemed to be buzzing, and it was suddenly unbearable to have this hanging over her. She snatched up the phone, called the hospital and left a message on Andrew's voice mail. He came back to her almost at once.

'Is Hetta all right?'

'She's fine. I called because some mail arrived for you.'

There was a short silence that would have told her the truth if nothing else had done.

'I'll be there this evening,' he said shortly, and hung up.

She replaced the receiver, and in that exact moment it came over her what a stupid thing she'd done. She could have screamed. By forcing this out into the open she'd made the place too hot to hold her, but she had nowhere else to take Hetta where she would be safe and happy. She should have endured anything rather than spoil things for Hetta. And she would have done, if she'd stopped to think.

I don't learn, she castigated herself bitterly. *Act first, talk first, and think afterwards, when it's way too late. Just like then.*

She could simply have sent the envelope on to the hospital. Andrew would have guessed what she knew when he opened it, but he could have turned a blind eye. Now she'd forced him into the open.

She would have given anything to turn the time back ten minutes.

Or twelve years.

Still in a daze she wandered out into the garden, where Hetta was piling pebbles on top of each other with fierce concentration, until they collapsed.

'It's lovely having a garden, Mum. I do like it here.'

So did I, she thought. *It was like the Garden of Eden. But now the serpent's poisoned everything.*

'Let's go back in,' she said in a strained voice. 'You mustn't overdo it.'

By ten o'clock that night he hadn't shown up, and there was no message. Ten became eleven. Midnight passed.

It meant nothing. There was an emergency at the hospital.

And he wouldn't think to call me, she thought wryly. *Because he sees only the straight path ahead. No distractions. Why am I such a fool?*

The call came the next morning while she was serving breakfast. As she had thought, it had been an emergency.

'I was going to let you know,' he said, sounding tired. 'But things were desperate. I couldn't call you myself and I—didn't want anyone else to do it. I'll be there tonight, if that's OK?'

She assured him that it was fine. To be on the safe side she went out and bought a newspaper with details of rooms to let. And that evening it was the same, hour following hour with no sign of him. So now she knew where she stood. But why? she wondered despondently. Why be kind and then snub her like this? For the pleasure of it?

When she'd put Hetta to bed she sat downstairs for a long time, trying to make herself do something decisive, but lacking the energy. The world seemed cold and dreary.

Suddenly it was one in the morning. She'd been staring into space for more than two hours. She pulled herself together and went out into the hall to mount the stairs. As she did so, a brilliant light shone through the door window, almost blinding her. There was the sound of a car engine, then the slamming of the door. And finally the doorbell.

It couldn't be Andrew, because he must have a key.

But it was Andrew, frowning and uneasy.

She stood back to let him pass, closed the door behind him and helped him off with his coat.

'I'm sorry to be so late,' he said. 'If I hadn't seen the lights on I'd have left. I've been operating all evening.'

'Then you'd better have something to eat,' she said. She needed time to sort out her thoughts. His face was exhausted and haggard, and he looked so different from the man she'd been picturing that she felt the ground shaking under her feet.

'Just a snack. Don't go to any trouble.'

'Omelette,' she said, heading for the kitchen. 'I've got plenty of milk.'

'Fine, I'll have some.'

She filled a tall glass with milk, and watched him drink it. 'Johnny used to say you drank so much milk because you were preparing for your first ulcer,' she remembered suddenly.

'Yes,' he said, as though the memory had surprised him. 'So he did.'

After that she turned away suddenly to concentrate on the omelette. He asked how Hetta was progressing, and mentioned her next appointment, and in this way they got through the next few minutes.

He ate like a man too tired to know what he was putting into his mouth.

'When did you last eat?' Elinor asked.

'Staff canteen. Lunchtime.'

'Is one omelette enough?'

'Would you mind making another one?' he said at once.

She smiled. 'Of course not. Go into the other room, and I'll bring it in.'

A few minutes later she found him on the sofa. She set the plate down on a low table beside him and he smiled his thanks.

'I'm sorry to do this to you two nights running.'

'Don't be silly. Your patients come first. Was it another emergency?'

'No, the same one. A child. He was rushed in last night, and I thought—it looked like it would be all right. But tonight he took a turn for the worse. We did our best for him, but there was never really any chance.'

'I'm sorry.'

'Don't be,' he said harshly. 'It's part of the job. You just have to go on.' He gave a forced smile and indicated the food. 'This is good.'

'I've got some trifle. You should eat as much as you can.'

He gave a faint grin. 'Fattening me up?'

'You never got fat, whatever you ate. It used to make me so mad.'

'Yes. I know.' He added quickly, 'Some trifle, then.'

Another mine dodged. But still the minefields stretched ahead.

When he'd finished eating he yawned, then leaned his head back against the chair, eyes closed. She could clearly see the shape and line of each feature. The straight, uncompromising nose, the strong chin that could only have belonged to a stubborn man, and the mouth that somehow didn't fit with the rest of the face. It was expressive, mobile, suggesting sensitivity, although it had hardened somewhat since they'd loved each other years ago. There were two deep lines on either side of it now, and more lines at the corners of his eyes. It was the face of a man who spent most of his life being tired, and refusing to admit it.

For years she'd resisted the memory of his kisses, and her own frustrated desire for him. But the really dangerous memory was more recent. Just a few short weeks ago his arms had held her as he'd soothed her sobs in the hospital garden. She could feel him now, drawing her head against his shoulder, murmuring soft words of comfort, and against this memory she had no defence at all.

The mouth that now lay relaxed might, or might not, have kissed her hair that night. She couldn't be sure. At the time she'd had no thought for anything but Hetta. It was only afterwards, reliving the moment, that she'd thought she'd felt the soft pressure of his lips. Or maybe not.

His eyes opened so slowly that she had time to avert her gaze, but she didn't try. Nor did he. He only looked at her sadly, and his mouth quirked wryly as though he could see a joke against them both.

'I still can't believe this,' he said. 'And perhaps it isn't really true.'

'That's how I've felt,' she admitted. 'Since that first day when I saw you in the hospital corridor—I tried not to believe it. I've always wondered what I would say to you if we met again, but in twelve years I've never found the answer. "I'm sorry" sounds so inadequate.'

'Good grief! Skip that! I hate apologies. I don't know how to make them myself and it embarrasses me when other people try. Could I have a cup of coffee?'

Domestic tasks were useful for getting over the awkward moments. She made some fresh coffee and when she returned he was studying the newspaper, open at the 'To Let' page, that she'd left on the sofa.

'It was stupid of me to think that you wouldn't find out.'

'This *is* your house?'

'Yes.'

'And Mr Martin?'

'He doesn't exist.'

'So it was all you, including the money you've been paying into my account?'

He shrugged. 'You really are doing me a favour by occupying the house. I don't like it to be empty.'

'You could have employed a house sitter for a quarter of the price. This was just a device for—for—'

'Helping out an old friend?'

'Is that what you call it? To me it looks like charity.'

He frowned. 'Are you angry with me?'

To her own dismay, she found that she was. She'd resolved to play it cool, but she'd reckoned without the humiliation that burned in her when she thought of living on his handouts.

'It doesn't matter,' she said hastily, trying to control herself.

'It matters to me. As I said, it was for an old friend—'

'We were never friends,' she flashed.

'No, we were lovers, until the day you found another lover that you preferred. But you had every right to do that, and if I can draw a line under it, why can't you?'

'Because you've been giving me money,' she said. 'It's—it's insulting.'

'I didn't mean to insult you. I just did what I thought you needed.' He gave a grunt of laughter. 'One thing hasn't changed. You always had a genius for putting me in the wrong. I never knew where I was. I suppose that was part of your charm.'

She'd pulled herself together. 'It's only charming in a seventeen year old,' she said. 'In a middle-aged woman it's a pesky nuisance.'

'You're not middle-aged,' he said quickly. 'You're not even thirty.'

'I look forty and I feel fifty.' She sighed. 'But I'm acting like a ten year old, aren't I? I'm sorry, Andrew. It's just that there's something about taking money—'

'Will you drop the subject?' He sounded strained.

'Yes.' Casting around for another subject, she said brightly, 'Your house is wonderful.'

'Is it?' He sounded barely interested.

'You know it is. You did it. You got where you said you wanted. I always knew you would.'

'Is that what this place says to you? Success?'

'Of course. And the car.'

'Oh, yes. I never knew that my character included a strain of the flashy and vulgar until I found I could afford the toys to play with. And I enjoyed them for a while. I still enjoy the car.' He shook his head as though trying to clear it. 'Forgive me.'

'Forgive you?'

'For not telling you the truth. I meant it for the best, but I should have known that you wouldn't want anything to do with it.' He shrugged. 'Well, anyway—there's no need for this.' He indicated the paper.

'I thought you'd want me to go when I found out.'

'Why should I?'

'Because you took so much trouble to stop me knowing.'

He gave a faint grin, directed at himself. 'You don't know the half of it. I came back here that night and went through the place, hiding anything that could have betrayed me. I stocked the freezer from an all-night supermarket about a mile away. Then I had my phone calls redirected, and my mail rerouted—not that much usually comes here anyway. I did anything I could think of.'

'But why?'

'Would you have accepted if you'd known it was me?'

'I wouldn't have wanted to,' she said after a moment's thought. 'But I'd have had no choice.'

'Exactly. You'd have come here reluctantly, been

horribly embarrassed, and got out as soon as you could. I didn't want that.'

'Was that why you knocked on the door tonight instead of using your key?'

'I don't have a key. That is—I do, but not on me. It's locked in my desk, in the study here. This is your house, while you need it. You couldn't feel like that if I could come and go here without your permission.'

'Andrew, I'm sorry,' she said impulsively. 'I backed you into a corner about this, but I never meant to.'

'What do you mean, backed me into a corner?'

'When you found me having hysterics in the garden that night, it was a kind of emotional blackmail.'

'I never felt that. I just felt that I wanted to help you. I couldn't tell you the truth because I knew I wasn't your favourite person.'

'Shouldn't that be my line? I gave you every reason to hate me.'

'I've never hated you, Ellie. Well, yes, perhaps at the beginning. I was young then, and my pride had been hurt. Pride's damnably important when you're twenty-six. But I recovered my sense of proportion. It's a great leveller, a sense of proportion. It helps you see that the things that once seemed earth-shattering didn't matter so much after all. Certainly not enough to hate someone.'

'I'm glad,' she said quietly.

'And you did me a favour. I wasn't ready to marry. I still had my way to make.'

'I seem to recall your mother warning you about that at the time,' Elinor said.

'Yes, and I wouldn't listen. Which was stupid of

me.' Abruptly he changed the subject. 'Are you taking care of yourself?'

'I'm all right. Hetta's the sick one.'

'No, Hetta's the recovering one. If you're not careful you're going to be the sick one. The strain on you has been enormous. You've been fighting to be strong, for her, but who's strong for you?'

Only you, she thought. *Ever. But I can't say that.*

'Just make sure you look after yourself now,' he said firmly. 'You need to heal as well.'

'Well, this is the right place to do it,' she agreed. 'Where are you living? I haven't forced you to move into a hotel, have I?'

'No, I've got a little place near the hospital. I'm used to spending most of my time there. I bought this house for my wife, a few years ago.'

'Your—wife?'

'Until recently. The divorce was finalised a few weeks back. I offered her the house as part of the settlement, but she preferred money, so I still have it. I'll get around to selling it soon.'

'Perhaps it still means something to you?'

'No, I'm not clinging onto ''happy memories''. There aren't any. We knew it was a mistake fairly soon, and the end was always inevitable. All we've had in common for years has been our son. It was a ''good'' marriage, but not a happy one.'

'Good?'

'Suitable for a young man with his way to make. I wanted to get onto Elmer Rylance's team because he was the best heart surgeon in the world. Half the techniques in use today were invented, or at least perfected, by him. I could have learned them from others, but that wasn't good enough for me. Only the master would do. Lord, I was conceited in those days!

'The difficulty was, getting myself noticed among so many competing for his attention. Then I met Myra at some medical charity function. She's his niece.'

'Oh, I see,' Elinor said quietly.

'Yes, it was as cynical and planned as that. Not the first meeting. That was accident. But dancing with her, trying to turn her head, establishing myself as her escort, all that was done with a purpose. Not very attractive behaviour, but it's the way the world works. At least it does for a certain kind of man, and that was the kind of man I was. Nice, eh?'

'You're very hard on yourself. Why?'

'Because I like to face the truth, and the truth about myself isn't pretty. When I want something I go for it like a bulldozer, and I don't notice who I'm mowing down in the process. You of all people have reason to know that.'

The hint that he blamed himself for their past, rather than her, took her by surprise. She looked at him sadly, not knowing what to say.

'What happened to you afterwards?' he asked.

'I got married to Jack Smith, and it was a disaster. He was every bad thing you warned me about, and in my heart I knew it all the time.'

'Then why—?'

'Because I'd backed myself into a corner,' she said bitterly. 'I just couldn't admit I was wrong. You warned me he was a bad lot, so I had to marry him to prove he wasn't. But he was. After two years I gave up.'

'And Tom Landers?'

'He was my new start, a demonstration to the world

that I didn't foul up every time. Except that he was worse than Jack. Hetta was the only good thing to come out of our marriage. After that I swore no more men.'

'Very wise,' he mused. 'You were always a rotten picker.'

'Not always,' she said, and let it go at that.

CHAPTER EIGHT

ANDREW didn't answer and for a moment an awkward silence fell between them. It was broken by a squeak of delight from the hall and Elinor looked up to see Hetta bounding in.

'I knew you'd come to see me,' she said, jumping on Andrew.

'But of course I did,' he said, giving her a hug, and finding himself embracing Samson as well. 'Good grief, have you still got that revolting bear?'

'He's not a revolting bear,' she reproved. 'He's a nice bear. He stayed with me all the time, except when you were horrible and made him have a bath.'

'Yes, I remember now,' he said hastily. 'Beg pardon, ma'am.'

'Samson's my best friend.'

'Better than me?' He sounded piqued.

'Well—p'raps just a bit. But not much.'

Andrew grinned, and again Elinor marvelled at the change in him.

'What are you doing out of bed?' Elinor demanded, trying to sound severe.

'I had to come down and see Andrew 'cos he came to visit me.'

'Of course,' Andrew agreed.

'Can I have some milk?' Hetta begged, sounding like a starving orphan.

'Will you go straight back to bed afterwards?' Elinor countered.

'She's only just arrived,' Andrew protested.

'Andrew hasn't seen my scar yet.'

'And I haven't seen her scar yet.'

It dawned on Elinor that behind the humour he had a serious purpose. He wanted Hetta to stay for his own reasons: perhaps because he felt more at ease with another person there.

She went into the kitchen for milk, and returned to find the other two deep in discussion of medical matters. Hetta was displaying her scar with immense pride, while Andrew studied it and observed how well it had healed.

'How do you enjoy living here?' he asked.

'Heaps,' Hetta said at once. 'There's a huge garden and a swing, and—' her voice became blissful '—Mummy's here all the time.'

'I haven't been with her enough in the past,' Elinor said quickly. 'I had to work and it took me away a lot. But now we're together all day, just the two of us. As Hetta says, it's lovely.'

'I'm glad,' Andrew said. He looked back to Hetta. 'Do you still have those nightmares?'

'Not really,' she said in a considering tone. 'I have funny dreams with lots of things happening, but I'm not scared any more. Not since you told me about them.' She suddenly looked into his face. 'Do *you* have bad dreams?'

He flinched. 'Why do you ask that?'

'You look as if you do.'

'Hetta,' Elinor protested. 'Manners.'

Andrew was looking uncomfortable and it dawned on her that Hetta had touched a nerve. 'Well, everyone does sometimes,' he said. 'Now it's time you went back to bed. It's very late.'

'Will you tuck me up, and I can show you my room?'

'Darling—' Elinor said in quick dismay, but Andrew had already risen and taken the child's hand.

Elinor guessed that the bedroom had been his son's, but he might have been seeing it for the first time as he let Hetta show it to him. It was strange to watch them. Anyone seeing the three of them, not knowing the truth, would have thought them a perfect family. Hetta herself was overjoyed to have her friend back, blissfully ignorant of the undercurrents and tensions between the adults. And maybe her perspective was the right one.

At last she was asleep and they crept out and down the stairs.

'I must be going now,' Andrew said. 'Please don't think of leaving this house. I won't trouble you.'

'Is that what you think you are? A trouble to me? After what I owe you?'

'I wish you wouldn't talk about owing me. That isn't how I think of it. And I only meant that I'm not going to use your circumstances to force my presence on you. You can't go. She's happy. Don't take that away from her just because we once—because of things that don't matter any more.' He looked at her wryly. 'If they ever really mattered.'

'Didn't they?' she couldn't resist asking.

'I don't know. I don't think I can remember by now. Other things become important, other griefs can be greater, and suddenly you wonder what it was all about. But I know this. There's nothing in our past that should drive you away from here.'

'Thank you,' she said, trying to be as relieved as he plainly meant her to, but feeling only an ache. 'It's kind of you—' She stopped, her gaze fixed on his face. 'Andrew, you're dead on your feet. You can't keep your eyes open, can you?'

'I'll be all right. The night air will wake me up.'

'You won't be in the air, you'll be in the car, and you'll probably crash it.' As if to confirm her words he closed his eyes again. She took his arm and led him firmly back to the living room, and almost pushed him down onto the sofa.

'You were crazy coming out here so late after the day you've had. It could have waited until tomorrow.'

'No, it couldn't, not after I didn't turn up last night. I needed to talk to you, make you understand.'

'I understand that you're not fit to drive.'

'Perhaps if you made me a coffee—'

'The only thing I'm making for you is a bed. You're sleeping here.'

'Am I?'

'Yes. How much sleep did you get last night?'

'Three or four hours. I honestly don't remember.'

'Tell me which room.'

'The one with the pine door,' he said vaguely.

'Key.'

'It's on my keyring.'

'Which is?'

'In the drawer of my desk—in the study.' He seemed to be having trouble thinking of the words.

'And the key to that?' she persisted.

'Oh—yes.'

He felt in an inner pocket and produced some keys. Elinor located the one that opened the study, then the top drawer of the desk, and finally the complete set of house keys.

She found the pine door two along from Hetta's

room and opened it quietly. It didn't entirely surprise her to find that it was as plain as her own was ornate. The bed was narrow and looked hard. The furniture was neat and functional. Whatever Andrew had been like once, this was how he was now.

She remembered how he'd shrugged aside the child's death, with a brusque remark about 'going on'. He was right, but it had given her a chill to hear it put that way. Would he have taken Hetta's death so coolly? It was hard to believe, when he was so easy and friendly with her, but what did she know of him?

By the time she'd finished he'd appeared in the doorway. 'Thank you,' he said briefly.

'When do you want to be called?'

'I normally set my alarm for six, but I guess I can allow myself a little longer tomorrow. I'm not operating.'

'Goodnight, then.'

She finished clearing away downstairs and went up quietly. As always Hetta's door stood open, and she looked in, listening to the soft, even breathing, before going to her own room.

She lay down but sleep wouldn't come. Andrew's words, 'suddenly you wonder what it was all about,' haunted her. In her mind she had invested their meeting with so much significance, and now he'd told her, very kindly, that it meant nothing to him. He'd said, too, that she'd done him a favour by deserting him, freeing him to fulfil himself.

But that's not true, she thought, sitting up suddenly. *He was the one who was desperate to get married. I didn't look further than being in love. That's why I hurt him so much.*

'I couldn't help it,' she whispered now into the

darkness. 'You wanted me too much. I couldn't cope. Now you're coping by changing the past so that it didn't mean anything.'

She would try to believe that that was best for both of them, but the pain was still there. It was as though she'd possessed one glorious treasure in all her life. And he'd shown her that it was only made of lead.

It had been foolish of her to feel a brief stab of pleasure at the discovery that he was unmarried. What possible difference could that make to her?

But she couldn't hide from her own heart. Since they'd met she'd seen the man nature had meant him to be, not only brilliant but generous in a way that had gone far beyond the call of duty.

He'd loved her and she'd thrown it away. She'd refused to face her regret but it had always been there, and now there was no hiding from it.

Suddenly she sat up, alerted by an unfamiliar sound, as though someone were crying out. In an instant she was out of bed, hurrying across the corridor to Hetta. But her daughter's room was quiet, her sleep undisturbed. The sounds were coming from further down the hall.

Elinor crept out, closing Hetta's door so that she should hear nothing, and made her way along to the pine door. There was no doubt now that the cries were coming from the man who slept behind it, and she knew he wouldn't be pleased if she disturbed him. But she couldn't leave him like this. Pushing open the door, she slipped in and closed it behind her.

A soft light from the window limned his body. He wore no pyjama top, and the sheet had slipped down far enough for her to suspect that he probably wore nothing else either. Not wanting to embarrass him, she swiftly drew it higher, then dropped down by the bed and put her hands on his shoulders, shaking him hard.

'Andrew—Andrew—wake up.'

His eyes opened fast and immediately flew to the little clock beside him with its luminous figures.

'What is it?' he demanded hoarsely. 'Who needs me? Tell them I'm coming at once.'

'No.' She shook him again. 'There's no need for that.' She put the bedside lamp on. 'It's me, you're not in the hospital.'

His eyes seemed to take a moment to focus. Then she felt the tension drain out of him.

'Thank you,' he said wearily. 'Was I shouting?'

'Yes.'

'I'm sorry. It's abominable of me to disturb you. Hetta—?'

'She's still asleep.'

'Thank God! It's just something that happens now and then when I've been overworking.'

'I think you overwork all the time.'

He gave a mirthless laugh. 'Yes, par for the course. Sometimes it's worse than others, but it doesn't mean anything.'

'That's not true,' she said quietly. 'You know it isn't.'

She became aware that she was still holding him, and took her hands away. He hauled himself up in bed, grasping the sheet firmly, in a way that suggested her suspicions had been correct. Then he sat leaning against the bedhead with an expression that seemed strangely defeated. His hair was tousled and fell over his broad forehead.

'Some things are hard to cope with,' he said at last.

'That child who died tonight—we all fought so hard, but it was no use—' Suddenly he closed his eyes. 'He was six years old,' he said huskily.

She drew a swift breath. Who could empathise with that pain better than herself? But she could see the answer on Andrew's face. He was ravaged by his failure, and it was more than the damaged pride of a man who hated to fail. She was witnessing real misery.

'The worst thing is telling the parents,' he went on. 'They were so happy. They'd thought it was going to be all right, and then—their faces.'

'Must it be you who tells them?'

'Yes. I'm the one who's failed them, you see.'

'But that's not fair. People die. It's not your fault. You can't be held responsible if the odds are too great.'

'But I'm the one they trusted.' He gave her a swift, intent look. 'If Hetta had died, wouldn't you have felt that I'd let you down?'

'I know heart transplants are risky,' she said carefully, 'and it's not fair to blame the surgeon because luck was against him. I wanted a miracle and you gave it to me. But if not—I hope I'd have understood.'

'You wouldn't,' he said, smiling at her sadly. 'You mightn't have said anything, but you'd have looked at me—and I'd have seen you—'

'She's everything to me. You were our only hope and if things had gone wrong—yes, you're right. I wouldn't have been just or fair about it. What did the parents say to you?'

'Nothing. They just looked betrayed. And I can't wipe that look out of my mind. I wanted to be able to tell them that it was all a dreadful mistake, that

their son was alive and would wake up soon. I wanted
to promise them a miracle, but the miracles aren't in
my hands—' He closed his eyes.

'Andrew—' She reached out and touched him
again, gently. He opened his eyes and looked at her
with weary despair. 'I'm becoming afraid,' he whispered. 'And how can I work if I'm afraid?'

Never before had she known him admit to fear or
doubt. It broke down her defences, and without thinking whether she was being wise she gathered him into
her arms. Miracles weren't in her power either, or she
would have performed a dozen for him. She would
gladly have lifted the weights that were crushing him,
given him everything, even herself if that was what
he wanted.

She caressed him with passionate tenderness, murmuring anything she could think of to comfort him.
'You're not really afraid, my dear. It's only tiredness.'

'But it goes on and on,' he whispered. 'And there's
no rest. It's not the work, it's the responsibility—people's lives in your hands. That's the one thing I never
thought of in those days.'

'Those days,' she said longingly.

'Do you remember how it was then?' he murmured
against her hair. 'How confident I was—no, not just
confident, arrogant, cocky!'

'I thought it was wonderful,' she said with a remembering smile. 'You were like a king, so sure of
yourself.'

'But I shouldn't have been. I never saw the traps I
was laying for myself.'

'Nor did I,' she said gently. 'I don't suppose we
ever do.'

'Not until it's too late.' He rested his head against her.

'Do you have nights like this very often?' she asked, stroking his hair.

'Yes. That's one reason I started to stay at the flat. It's better to be alone when this happens.'

'No,' she said swiftly. 'It's never better to be alone. Haven't you learned that? I have.'

'How?'

'Through being alone,' she said simply.

'Funny. In all those years I never pictured you alone.'

His voice was so quiet that she had to strain to hear it. 'What—did you say?' she asked after a moment.

'You were so lovely and full of life—it was what drew me to you—I couldn't stay away—'

'Did you want to?'

'Yes. I kept trying to be strong, but it was no use.'

'I wish I'd known. I always thought of you as so aloof. Andrew?'

Silence. He had fallen asleep against her shoulder.

Moving very carefully, she swung her legs up onto the bed and lay down, drawing him beside her. He made a sound between a grunt and a sigh, turning slightly so that his weight was half across her, his head between her breasts. The bed was so narrow that she was forced to lie pressed up to him, intensely aware of his hard body, now relaxed against hers.

She held him lightly until he began to mutter again, and then she tightened her arms, whispering wordless comfort until the tension went out of him and he fell silent once more.

She stared into the darkness, thinking how achingly ironic it was that he should lie with her now, and not twelve years ago. Then her young body had clamoured for him. Now the ache of desire was there again, but tempered with understanding, and even compassion. She was no longer a girl thinking of her own wishes, but a woman who'd been through the mill and wanted to give him anything that would make his life sweeter.

When he moved again she kissed him, very softly and tenderly, and was pleased when he immediately calmed again. She kissed him again and felt his arms tighten.

'It's all right,' she whispered. 'I'm here.'

She didn't know if he could hear her but she murmured to him again, not words but wordless sounds of comfort, stroking her fingers gently against his hair, his face.

'This is how it should have been,' she told him softly. 'We should always have been like this—if only I'd understood—'

In her mind she saw again the time they'd landed on the little island and lain blissfully under the trees, until she'd broken their bliss by trying to claim him as a lover, and blaming him when he'd refused. Two selfish husbands had taught her the value of a man who'd loved her more than his own pleasure, a man she'd thrown away.

'You were thinking of me, but I didn't know it,' she murmured. 'And when I understood it was all too late. We had something so wonderful and special. I know it now. I used to tell you that I loved you but I didn't know what the words meant. But I could tell you now, if only I could be sure that you wanted to hear. Oh, darling, such things I could say to you now!'

He stirred again and she held her breath, wondering if he'd heard her. He seemed to be still asleep but his hands moved across her body. She should wake him now, and stop him doing this, but the excitement he was setting off confused her.

She wished that she were wearing something beautiful, a glamorous, flimsy concoction such as a woman chose for her lover. The nightgown she had on was made of cotton, and buttoned up to the neck. Its matronly style fitted the way she saw herself these days, but it was out of keeping with the fierce sensations that were coursing through her.

His fingers had found her buttons, were undoing the top one, then the next and the next. She did the rest herself, wrenching at them so fast that the last one flew off. It was she too who pulled the sheet back so that her nakedness lay next to his.

'Ellie...' The word was a whisper.

'Yes, darling, I'm here. Hold onto me.'

She clung to him too, kissing him without restraint, loving him with the pent-up love of years. 'Hold me,' she repeated.

His mouth covered hers eagerly. She welcomed him in, offering her whole self, keeping nothing back. Whatever he needed now, that was what she wanted to give.

He moved like a man urgently pursuing something he had long desired. His hands seemed to know instinctively how to find her, roving lovingly over the hills and valleys of her shape. Now she too was free to explore him and sense what she'd only suspected before, the power of him, the taut hardness of his muscles. He had been designed to please a woman, and everything in her responded.

He kissed her breasts, first one then the other, his tongue caressing her gently, teasing the nipples to peaks of desire. She'd never known that anything could feel this good. She was coming into her own, claiming what had always truly been hers. She reached for him.

And then Andrew raised his head. His eyes opened.

And with brutal suddenness the dream was over. She saw the shock in his face as he realised what was happening, heard his horrified cry of, 'My God, *no!*'

CHAPTER NINE

ANDREW wrenched himself out of Elinor's arms and for a moment he covered his eyes with his hand, as though engulfed by some feeling that was too much for him. Bitterly she realised that he couldn't even bear to look at her.

'Andrew—' she said desperately.

'No, for pity's sake! Ellie, this isn't the way I wanted it, can't you understand?'

'I'm sorry,' she said, scarlet with embarrassment. 'I didn't mean to—'

'It's my fault. I shouldn't have come here tonight. It's not fair on you.'

She could hear him talking fast, trying to put a different light on this, anything rather than admit that he'd found himself with a woman he didn't want. It was part of his kindness, she thought wretchedly, to try to make her feel better, but nothing could do that.

She was frantically buttoning up her nightdress, keeping her head down, but she was still aware of hasty movements as he covered his nakedness.

'Dear God!' she wept.

'Ellie, please believe me, I didn't come here for this. When I arrived tonight I was going to explain, and then leave. That would have been best for both of us, and I swear it's what I meant.'

'Stop, stop!' she said in an agony of shame. 'Do you think anything you say now can make it right? You're right, you shouldn't have come here. No, no,

I didn't mean that. It was my fault. I shouldn't have called you, I shouldn't have come to this house. I should have realised that ''Mr Martin'' was an invention. I'm not a child to believe in Santa Claus.'

'Don't blame yourself. It was something I wanted to do for you.'

'Why?' she demanded. 'Why should you do anything at all for me? You hate me. You have done for years.'

'I've never hated you.'

'Oh, no, you rise above that, don't you?' she raged. She didn't know why she was turning her temper on him, except that it made her pain more bearable. 'Simple revenge would be beneath you, but heaping coals of fire on my head is different. Was that what it was all about? Make me realise what I threw away? Make me really regret it? Was that the idea? Because if so it was unworthy of you.'

'Ellie, what is this?'

'You know very well what it's about. I really made a fool of myself, didn't I? Just like I did once before, remember, that day on the island? And you turned away from me then, too. You'd think I'd learn, wouldn't you?'

'That other time was different. There was love then. But this—'

'What about ''this''? I made a fool of myself again. Or did you make a fool of me? Because that makes us quits, doesn't it? After all this time you finally did it.'

'Stop it, for pity's sake!'

She didn't hear him. 'So let me tell you the rest, then you can really enjoy it. Jack Smith was a drunk who knocked me around, and Tom Landers was a control freak who walked out on me when Hetta was ill. And all the time I knew it was my own fault and I was being punished for what I did to you—'

His hand over her mouth cut her off. Nothing else would have done so. She was adrift in another world where there was only the sound of her own voice saying terrible things to silence her agony of embarrassment.

'You must be mad to talk like this,' he said, dropping his hand and taking her by the shoulders. 'What have I done to deserve it? You make me sound like a monster of spite, and if that's really what you think then I'm surprised you waste two seconds on me.'

'I didn't mean that,' she choked.

'I think you did. I think you're coming out with all the hostility you spared me twelve years ago. Maybe I really did have a lucky escape. Or maybe we both did.'

Silence. He dropped his hands. They stared at each other, aghast.

A shudder went through him. He moved away from her and spoke over his shoulder.

'Let's call it a day. We've both said things tonight that should never have been said, and we have to forget them. In fact we have to forget everything that's happened. It was a mistake to think we could meet each other as though the past didn't exist.'

'Yes,' she said bleakly.

He turned slightly, making a visible effort to pull himself together. 'I'm sorry for everything. You have enough to bear without me adding to it. Go back and get some sleep now. I apologise for disturbing you.'

'Please don't mention it,' she said politely.

Somehow she got out of the room. She made it

along the corridor to her own room, shut the door and sank onto the bed, overtaken by violent shivering. She was cold, so cold. If only she could cry. But no tears would come. She felt she'd cried her last tear long ago.

She meant to be downstairs first next day, but Andrew was there before her, in the kitchen, making coffee. He smiled briefly and set one before her.

'Thank you for letting me stay,' he said politely. 'I needed that sleep.'

He still looked jaded and she wondered how much sleep he'd managed to get after she'd left.

'You're really doing double duty, aren't you?' she managed to say. 'Isn't Sir Elmer back from the flu yet?'

'It turned nasty and he was away longer than we expected, but with any luck he'll be back this week. It'll give me a chance to catch up with my paperwork.'

'And your sleep,' she suggested.

'True. We're none of us at our best when we're overtired, but it's pointless to dwell on those times.'

He was shifting his armour firmly back in place, telling her to forget that she'd seen his weakness, that he'd briefly clung to her and then calamity had engulfed them both.

'Elinor, I want you to understand—'

'It's all right, I understand perfectly.'

'I don't think you do. You were very kind to me last night. You gave me a warmth and comfort I'd almost forgotten existed. But kindness can only go so far, and I never meant to make demands on you.'

'Andrew, please—'

'Wait, let me finish. Last night I said I wasn't going to use your troubles as an excuse to force my presence on you, and barely a few hours later—it was unforgivable of me, and I apologise for my behaviour.'

'It wasn't your fault,' she said in a dead voice. 'You were asleep.'

'I can't justify myself that easily. Because of Hetta, because I was the one lucky enough to be able to help her, you seem to feel that you owe me something, and that you had to repay it. I promise you that isn't so. You owe me nothing, and the last thing I would ever want is that kind of gratitude.'

He was subtly rewriting the facts. In this new version she hadn't thrown herself at him and earned his contempt. It was he who had imposed on her. She wondered if he thought he was making it easier for her. If so, he was wrong. She felt as though she were dying inside. She would have stopped him if she could, but she had no strength to move or speak.

'I promise you nothing like it will ever happen again,' he continued. 'You'll be glad to know that this will be my last visit.' He checked his watch. 'I must be going. Say goodbye to Hetta for me.'

'Let me fetch her. She'll hate it that she missed you.'

'I examined her last night and found her in good shape. The district nurse will continue to call—'

'That's not what I meant. You've been nice to her; she likes you. Let me fetch her.'

'No, I'm in a bit of a hurry.'

'Then come to see us again.'

'I don't think so,' he said harshly, closing his briefcase and not looking at her. 'I'm glad we got matters sorted out, but there's no need—I mean, it would be better if we didn't see each other again. Wouldn't it?'

'Yes,' she said sadly. 'Perhaps it would.'

She followed him into the hall where he put on his jacket, collected his briefcase and went to the door.

'Thank you again,' he said formally. 'I hope you keep well. Please remain here for as long as you wish.'

In a moment the door of his exquisite car had closed behind him, the engine purred into life, and he vanished down the winding drive. Elinor watched him go with a sense of desolation. She knew he'd finally shut a door on her.

As she turned back into the house she saw her daughter descending the stairs slowly. Hetta's face showed that she'd seen him go.

'He didn't wait, Mummy,' she said in a voice of disillusion.

'No, darling. He couldn't.'

'Doesn't he like us after all?'

'He likes you to bits,' Elinor said, giving Hetta a hug. 'Now come on, let's have breakfast.'

For the first time ever her daughter's company was a strain. She wanted to be alone to think, and to cry. But somehow she got through the day without Hetta suspecting anything amiss, and then it was evening and she could go to her room, shut the door, and give way to her anguish.

If only she could blot out the sight of his eyes when he'd opened them, his horror when he'd seen who had been in his arms, his appalled cry of *'No!'* Perhaps he had another woman now, one he loved. And he'd awoken to find himself in the arms of a woman he hadn't chosen, one he now probably despised. That thought made her curl herself up into a tight little ball, as though by doing so she could vanish from her own eyes.

How could she have thought that she had anything to attract him now? But she hadn't been thinking of herself, only of him and his needs, and she'd opened her arms to him in defenceless love.

Love. She resisted the word, but it wouldn't let her go. It was too late now to protest that her love should never have been allowed to live again.

For it didn't live again. It had never died. Through twelve lonely years it had hidden away in a place she couldn't bear to visit, calling to her with a voice she'd refused to hear, waiting for the day it could seize her again. And this time there would be no escape.

After a few days she no longer strained her ears for the sound of a car. He wasn't coming back, and she couldn't stay here. Hetta was well enough for a move, and Andrew's generosity meant that she had enough money to cushion them for a while. It galled her to have to rely on his money, but at least she wouldn't accept any more.

She called Daisy, living in a comfortable little hotel near the boarding house, now being rebuilt. The hotel would have a twin room vacant next week, and Daisy reserved it for them. Hetta was in two minds over the move, sad to be leaving, but glad to see Daisy again.

She wrote Andrew a polite letter, thanking him for his kindness but explaining that she could no longer impose on him. She ended it, 'Yours sincerely, Elinor Landers (Mrs).'

In return she received a blunt note saying, 'There's no need for this. You should reconsider. A.'

She wrote back, 'Thank you, but my mind is made up. Elinor Landers.'

There was no reply.

The days began to narrow down. Four days, then three, then two, one. She would be gone soon and the last connection between them broken. Hetta would need one more visit to the hospital, but doubtless Andrew would depute another doctor to see her.

On the last day, while Hetta was upstairs, unpacking and repacking some toys for the umpteenth time, Elinor went around the garden, trying to be strong-minded and not let herself feel wretched. She knew she'd done the right, the only thing, but the voice of the tempter whispered that she could have stayed a little longer, and perhaps seen him just once more.

Then she thought how that meeting would be: full of the remembered humiliation of their last encounter. Was that pain worth it, just to see him one more time?

Yes, anything was worth it.

As she headed back to the house Elinor became aware that there was someone else in the garden. It was a tall, dark-haired woman, expensively dressed and with an air of ease that came from always having money. Elinor had seen that look often enough in her customers. The stranger watched her approach, unabashed at being discovered intruding. A few feet away Elinor stopped and the two women regarded each other.

'Who are you?' they both said.

The woman laughed. 'I'll answer first, although I don't know why I should, since it's my home.'

'This—? You're—?'

'I'm Myra Blake. And I should have said this *used* to be my home. I moved most of my things out months ago. It doesn't really bother me who's here now, but, just for the record, who are you?'

'I'm Elinor Landers,' she said carefully.

'And when did Andrew move you in? I must say, this kind of caper isn't normally in his line. Too much of a puritan. In fact, that's what—well, it's old history.'

'I'm only here because he operated on my little girl,' Elinor hastened to say, 'and while she was in hospital our home burned down. I had nowhere else to go, and he was very kind.'

Myra Blake gave a crack of laughter. 'Oh, yes, of course. I was forgetting how often he takes in waifs and strays from the hospital.' Her voice was heavy with irony.

'Mrs Blake, I promise you this isn't how it looks. Besides I shall be l—'

'Good grief, what do I care how it looks? Let's go inside and you can make me some tea.'

She turned and led the way to the house, the picture of confidence. Elinor followed, her head in a spin. But since Myra Blake wasn't flustered by the situation she determined that she wouldn't be either.

She made tea and carried it into the room overlooking the garden where Myra had removed her luxurious cashmere coat and tossed it onto a chair. She'd seated herself on the sofa and now leaned back, surveying Elinor from dark eyes that gleamed with malicious fun. She was lovely, with black shining hair, cut elegantly and just touching her shoulders. As a beautician Elinor had become a connoisseur of other women's looks, and professionally she had to admire Myra. Her legs were long and elegant, sheathed in black silk and ending in impossibly high heels. Her curvaceous figure looked as though she worked hard keeping it trim, her complexion was perfect and her face had been made up with great skill.

So this woman had been Andrew's wife, had shared his life, his home, his bed. He'd said it hadn't been a happy marriage, even implied that he'd married cynically, but at some point he must surely have been enraptured by her beauty, and whispered words of passion into her ears as they'd danced at their wedding.

'Smashing!' Myra said suddenly, and Elinor stared at hearing the down-to-earth word from this picture of elegance. 'Smashing tea! Best I ever tasted.' She was sipping enthusiastically.

'I'm glad you like it, Mrs Blake,' Elinor said politely, seating herself.

'Myra, please.'

'Myra, there's a lot I don't understand.'

'Like how I just managed to walk in? I still have a key.' She leaned forward to put her cup on the low table, but suddenly she stopped, frowning as she looked at Elinor. 'Have we ever met before?'

'No, never.'

'Funny, you look familiar somehow. Never mind. So what am I doing here? I want to collect a few things that I left. And I thought Andrew might be around somewhere, although I can't imagine why. He never *was* around. I need to talk to him. So come on, tell me. What gives?'

'What gives?'

'You and Andrew.'

'There is no me and Andrew,' she said firmly. 'My daughter needed a heart transplant. She was originally a patient of Sir Elmer Rylance.'

'My uncle,' Myra said casually.

'Yes, I know.'

'Andrew told you that much, then. Go on.'

'He was ill when a heart became available for my daughter, so Andrew did the operation. And, as I told you, my home caught fire—'

'And he played the Good Samaritan. Well, well!' Myra was looking her over with a look that was hard to read, amused, cynical, but not unfriendly.

'It's a wonderful place for Hetta,' Elinor urged. 'So quiet and peaceful, which is what she needs to re-cover—'

'And Andrew here to keep an eye on her.'

'He doesn't live here,' Elinor said quickly.

'But he visits?'

'Only once to see how we were doing. It's just Hetta and me. He says he has this little apartment near the hospital—'

'Oh, sure, I know it. A real monk's cell. He spent most of his time there even when we were officially together. When he did come back it was just to see Simon, our son. Don't look like that. I don't suppose I'm telling you anything you didn't know. Andrew's obviously discussed me with you. Hell, I don't mind! In fact it rather suits me. Did he tell you I was getting married again?'

'No.'

'Well, I am. Cyrus Hellerman from Detroit. He's big in motors, and I mean *big*.'

'A millionaire?'

'Please! A million dollars gets you nowhere these days. Multi-multi-multi, if you know what I mean.'

'I think I do,' Elinor said. 'This wasn't enough, then?' She indicated the house.

'This? Nice little cottage, but I felt the need to spread my wings. Enter Cyrus. His wife had died a few months back, he was lonely, and why hang around?'

'For someone else to snap him up?'

'Right,' Myra said, unabashed. 'Of course, Andrew is very successful in his way, and when I married him I was really in awe of him. Uncle Elmer said he was the best of his generation, but he had some funny ideas. He's never made as much money as he should have done because he does so much for free. Well, I respect that. I really do. But it got kind of boring when I wanted to remodel the house.'

'What did Uncle Elmer say about his unpaid work?'

'He was all for it. Said it enhanced Andrew's reputation.'

'But if he was helping people for nothing surely he was thinking of them, not himself?'

'Oh, please! I got all that high-minded stuff from him. I can't tell you how desperate I was to get away from it.' She looked at Elinor suspiciously. 'Are you high-minded?'

'Andrew has just saved my daughter's life, so I'm bound to be a bit high-minded about what he does.'

'Uh-huh! Well, I guess you can't help it, then,' Myra said, as though excusing some social flaw. 'I'm not that way myself.'

'But don't you come from a medical family?'

'Yes, and I can't tell you how that stuff got on my wick all these years. Andrew briefly made me find it acceptable, but the fact is that I misread him as he misread me, and the best thing we ever did was get a divorce.'

'But what about your son?'

'I'm coming to him. You could do me a favour.'
She spoke as though it were a given that Elinor would
want to. 'Simon is seven years old. What about your
little girl?'

'Seven too. And thanks to Andrew she's going to
be eight, and nine, and ten.'

'Uncle Elmer says he's the best surgeon he knows
for operating on young children. It's a special skill,
because everything's so small. Oddly enough, he's
good at talking to them as well.'

'Why is that odd?'

'Because his own son is a closed book to him.
Mind you, it would help if he spent some more time
with him.'

'But there must be so many demands on him.
Surely he manages as much as he can.'

'What do you know about it? Were you there on
Simon's fifth birthday? Or his sixth, come to that.
Have you seen the look on that child's face when his
father has put him last yet again? Andrew's digging
the grave of that relationship, and if I was the bitch
some people think I am I'd sit back and let him do
it. As it is, I'm here to do him a favour.'

CHAPTER TEN

MYRA waited for an answer to this last remark, but Elinor decided to play it safe with silence. She was apprehensive about the 'favour' Myra was proposing to do for Andrew. To her relief Myra didn't pursue the point.

'What do you think of this house?' she asked, going to look out of the window to where the garden was at its best.

'I love it.'

'Where are you sleeping?'

Dangerous ground. 'Well, I—'

'I expect you're in my room. It's a hoot, isn't it? That was my Victorian period, except for the bathroom, which was my Egyptian period. If I'd stayed on here I'd have changed them both. Is your daughter around now?'

'She's upstairs,' Elinor said, disconcerted by the abrupt change of subject. 'Oh, no, I think that's her.'

There was a noise in the hall, and the next moment Hetta wandered in, a toy in each hand, and with a cheerful smile that brightened as she saw a visitor.

'Come here, darling,' Elinor called.

Hetta came to her side and stood regarding the visitor with a wide-eyed stare that would have disconcerted someone less at ease than Myra.

'I'm Myra,' she said. 'I used to live here, and I've just been making friends with your mummy.'

'How do you do?' Hetta said politely.

'Do you like it here?'

Hetta nodded.

'Must be a bit lonely, though,' Myra suggested. 'No kids of your own age. No animals. Do you like dogs?'

Hetta nodded again with unmistakable eagerness.

'Then you'd get on well with my son, Simon. He's your age and he's got a puppy. Care to meet him?'

'And the puppy?' Hetta asked at once.

'And the puppy.' Myra flicked open a cell phone and spoke into it. 'OK, Joe.'

Elinor's suspicions were rising by the minute. 'Now, wait a moment—'

'You don't mind my son meeting your daughter, do you?' Myra asked with a touch of wide-eyed reproach.

'It's not that—'

'I really think they'll like each other, and it would mean a lot to him. Ah, there you are, darling!'

A boy of Hetta's age, accompanied by a uniformed chauffeur, had appeared in the door. Elinor drew a slow breath. This was a younger version of Andrew, not in his looks, which were more like Myra's, but in the stillness with which he held himself, the way he looked around the room, taking everything in, but saying nothing.

'This is Simon,' Myra said.

Elinor went forward to him. 'Hallo, I'm—I'm Ellie.' What had made her say that?

'How do you do?' he said politely. He started to offer his hand and remembered that he was holding the puppy. Hetta was there in a flash to relieve him of it.

Elinor introduced them. They were cautious about

each other, but the puppy was an immediate bond and after a moment they drifted into a corner together. Elinor could see that Hetta was delighted, and so could Myra. She was watching them with a satisfied expression.

'This is just perfect,' she said. 'All right, Joe, go and get yourself something to eat in the village. I'll call you when I need you.'

The chauffeur nodded and departed.

'Do you mean,' Elinor asked, outraged, 'that you've kept your son sitting out there in the car while you came in here to—to—?'

'Survey the land,' Myra said. 'Of course. It wouldn't have been very nice to bring him in before I knew what he might find, would it? I brought him with me just in case the things I'd heard about you were true. Be prepared, that's my motto.'

'And just what have you heard about me?'

'That you had a kid of your own, same age as Simon, and that you were a good mother. Looks true to me. Otherwise I'd just have taken him away again.'

'Myra, what have you got in mind?'

'Well, my life is getting a bit complicated. Cyrus wants to get married in the next couple of weeks because of some motor show or other, and I need to get out there fast.'

'So take Simon with you.'

'On my honeymoon? Get real. Besides, it's time Andrew really made an effort with his son. It's always been too easy for him to duck out. This time he isn't going to.'

'And you're just going to dump him?' Elinor demanded, speaking quietly, lest Simon heard.

Instead of answering direct Myra said, 'Nurse

Stewart's been talking. I gather it was a bit like a French farce that night, you skulking in Andrew's office or under a blanket in the back seat of his car. That bit didn't come from Stewart, but from someone in the parking lot. And one of the district nurses knows this house is Andrew's. I have friends at the hospital and they've kept me informed. It all became very intriguing and I got curious. It's so unlike him.'

'You mean I've made a scandal for him? Oh, no!'

'I suppose it is potentially scandalous,' Myra mused. 'Of course, you're not Andrew's patient but your daughter is, and all this dodging around in car parks is something his enemies could make something of. Andrew's got a lot of enemies. Brilliant people always do, and especially now that Uncle Elmer's heading for retirement. His illness took a lot out of him, so he'll probably go quite soon now. The contenders are lining up to take his place, and malicious tongues are all ready to wag.'

Elinor listened to this with mounting horror. She'd never meant to harm Andrew, but that was what she seemed to have done. But Myra, watching her, gave a cheeky smile.

'Don't worry, *I'm* not malicious, and I won't make trouble. My word on it, and you really can trust my word. I may be superficial and tinselly—guess who called me that?—but when I make a promise I keep it.'

For some reason Elinor believed her.

'But why are you being like this?' she asked. 'I don't understand.'

'You mean why aren't I jealous that he moved another lady in here?'

'You've nothing to be jea—'

'Skip it. You'd have expected a fit, jealous or otherwise. Sorry. Can't oblige. Oh, there was a time when I thought the sun shone out of Andrew, but that was before I discovered what a bore he was.'

'A bore? Andrew?' The exclamation was jerked out of Elinor.

'There, I knew you were high-minded!' Myra exclaimed as though she'd scored a victory. 'Good luck to you. Actually this rather suits me.'

Elinor pulled herself together. This woman's determination to arrange life to suit herself had a hypnotic quality.

'I'm sorry, but you're under a misapprehension,' she said firmly. 'Hetta and I are leaving tomorrow.'

'Damn! Have you and Andrew quarrelled?'

'No,' Elinor said stiffly.

'Has he thrown you out?'

'No.'

'Then why are you leaving?'

'Because Hetta is greatly improved and it's time to move on.'

'Why?'

'I'm sorry, I can't discuss that with you.'

'Where are you going?'

'I don't see why I should dis—'

'Oh, nonsense, of course you can. This is important. Have you got somewhere better than this?'

'No, we're going to a small hotel where I have a friend living. She owned the boarding house that burned down but it'll soon be rebuilt so—'

'You're dumping Andrew for a boarding house? C'mon! Stay here. It's much nicer.'

'That's not the point,' Elinor said, feeling desperate. It was like trying to argue with a juggernaut.

'Even if I weren't going you couldn't just leave Simon here without telling Andrew first.'

'Then let's tell him. You call him up while I make us something to eat.'

Elinor watched helplessly as Myra whisked herself into the kitchen and set about preparing. There was no doubt she was the expert cook for whom the place had been created. She started with milk shakes for the children, who downed them eagerly.

'Go in the garden, kids, and I'll have something more filling for you in a minute,' she called. To Elinor she said, 'Go on, get calling.'

There was nothing to do but obey, although she flinched at the thought of calling a man who'd made it so clear that she embarrassed him. She used the hall phone, and in a few moments she heard Andrew's voice, terse, commanding. 'Yes?'

'It's me,' she said. 'I'm sorry to disturb you at work but something's happened.'

'Hetta?'

'No, Myra, your ex-wife. She's here, and she's got Simon with her. And I think she means him to stay when she goes.'

'I don't understand.'

'She's going to America to get married, and she's not taking him.'

'Put her on,' he snapped.

Elinor returned to the kitchen. 'Andrew wants to talk to you.'

'Sorry, I'm too busy.'

'You can't be. It's what you came here for.'

'No way. I didn't come here for a phone conversation with Andrew. I can do that anywhere. Where's the raspberry sauce? You've moved it.'

'Top shelf. Please come and talk to him.'

'Nope. It was handier on the middle shelf.'

'Not for me. Hetta doesn't like it.'

'Simon adores it with ice cream and milk shake. I'll have some sent to you, but don't let him make a pig of himself. Better get back to Andrew.'

Elinor gave up and returned to the hall. 'She won't come,' she told Andrew.

She could hear him grinding his teeth. 'Tell her—'

She returned to Myra and spoke in a carefully expressionless voice. 'He says stop playing damn fool games and pick up the phone.'

Myra gave a rich crow of laughter. 'Don't worry, I won't embarrass you by responding in kind.'

To Elinor's relief Myra went out into the hall. But she merely hung up the phone and returned to the kitchen. 'No point in arguing,' she explained airily. 'He just doesn't listen.'

The telephone immediately rang and Elinor raced to snatch it up. 'It's not my fault,' she said, harassed.

'I know that. All right, please tell her I'll be over this evening. Are you all right? Is she making herself unpleasant?'

'No,' Elinor said wryly. 'I think she's a little crazy, but not unpleasant.'

She found Myra in the garden with the children, who were playing with the puppy. She had a moment to watch them unobserved, and hear Hetta's giggles of glee.

Then Myra hailed her. 'You stay here while I finish doing the eats,' she said. 'I'll yell when I'm ready.' She headed back to the house.

'Mummy, look at the puppy,' Hetta called. 'His name's Fudge.'

'That's because he's that pale brown colour,' Simon put in.

Fudge promptly squatted on the ground and produced an enormous puddle.

'He's nervous at being in a new place,' Simon hurried to say. 'And he's out in the garden. He *is* house-trained.' Honesty made him add, 'Well, sort of.'

She felt sad for the child, feeling the need to placate her. This was more his house than hers. What sort of a life had he had, between a distant father and the selfish, manipulative mother?

Hetta and Simon were already at ease with each other. He seemed to be a quiet, gentle child, and she couldn't help realising that he would be the ideal playmate for Hetta. She, for her part, had already given him the ultimate token of friendship, hauling up her T-shirt and displaying her wound with enormous pride. Simon had been suitably impressed.

At last Myra called, 'Come and get it!' and they all trooped to the house where she'd laid the table out on the patio.

The meal was a roaring success. Myra was skilled and imaginative, and she knew how to appeal to children. It was hard to dislike her. She was a tough cookie, who seemed to have little in the way of finer feelings. But she was good-natured, and had an outgoing quality that made her company pleasant for a while. Elinor guessed she liked everyone around her to be happy, and would even put herself out to achieve it—as long as she was sure of getting her own way in the end.

She also had a gift for telling a funny story. Despite her unease about Andrew's imminent arrival, Elinor found herself smiling at the tale of Fudge and a donkey. The children hooted with laughter.

They were like that when Andrew came in.

He'd meant to ring the front doorbell, but finding the side gate to the garden open he'd walked around the house until he'd heard laughing voices. Nobody heard him arrive, and he had a moment to stand, taking in the cheerful scene in which he had no part.

It was Elinor who saw him first, glancing up just before he controlled his expression. She rose and the movement alerted the attention of the others. Hetta beamed. Myra regarded him with a cynical smile. Simon looked pleased but uncertain what to expect. Andrew gave a brief nod in his direction, and an even briefer smile. Unease radiated from him.

'Good evening, Myra,' he said.

'You're just in time for some coffee, Andrew. Let's go in, it's getting a little chilly.'

When they had all moved into the living room Myra said, 'Kids, why don't you go and watch television upstairs?'

'I'll go too,' Elinor said hastily.

'Better if you stay,' Myra observed. 'Andrew and I can only take so much of each other's company undiluted.'

Elinor looked at Andrew. 'Please stay,' he requested.

When the children had gone upstairs, clutching Fudge, the three of them surveyed each other uneasily. Elinor felt almost overwhelmed by the bittersweet shock of Andrew's presence after she had accepted that she would never see him again. But she tried to keep a clear head, sensing she was going to need all her wits about her in the next few minutes.

'Myra, if you've come to make trouble—' Andrew began.

'But I haven't. When did I ever make trouble?'

'I won't answer that.'

'When you two have finished quarrelling, it's the kids' bedtime, and I need to know where Simon's sleeping,' Elinor said firmly.

'But here, of course,' Myra said sweetly. 'In his father's house.'

'With no warning?' Andrew snapped. 'You must be out of your mind.'

'Well, it's very simple. I'm off to Detroit to marry Cyrus, and really I can't take a little boy on my honeymoon, even if he wanted to come, which he very sensibly doesn't. He's thrilled at the thought of staying with you. You've let him down so often, but not this time.'

'Do you think I have time to care for a child?'

'Not you. Your girlfriend.'

'Ellie—Mrs Landers—is not my girlfriend, as you so vulgarly put it.'

'Nothing vulgar in having a girlfriend. It's about time you thought of something other than a scalpel.'

'If anybody's interested, I am leaving tomorrow morning,' Elinor said desperately.

'No, you're not,' Myra said airily. 'We settled all that.'

'Did we?' Elinor asked blankly.

'Be nice to her, Andrew. She's going to get you out of a hole.' She turned to Elinor. 'You don't mind getting him out of a hole, do you, Ellie? I can call you Ellie, can't I?'

'No,' Andrew said harshly.

Myra became businesslike. 'Look, it's very simple.

Simon is going to stay with you for a while. He's here now, he's got all his stuff, and he's looking forward to it. But if you refuse, then I'll take him away with me now, and he'll come with me to Detroit, and he'll stay there. For good. I swear you'll never see him again.'

He stared at her in a fury. 'You're bluffing.'

'I'm doing you a favour, forcing you to engage with your son before it's too late. So what happens? Do I take him away from you for good?'

'You know I won't let you do that.'

'Fine. He stays here.'

'You've already heard Mrs Landers say that she's leaving,' Andrew said in a tight voice.

'Then you'll have to persuade her to stay, won't you? I'm making some more coffee. Anybody want some?' She floated into the kitchen, as much at ease as though this were a social occasion.

Andrew could hardly look at Elinor.

'What do you want me to do?' she asked.

'I can't let her take him away for good, but if you leave she'll do that,' he said harshly.

She hesitated, torn. 'I don't think she really means that bit.'

'When she makes a threat she carries it out. *Help me, Ellie, for God's sake!*'

'But what use can I be?'

'Stay here. Let him live with you and Hetta.'

'But it's you he wants.'

'I'll visit as often as I can.'

'That's not enough.'

He met her eyes. 'Then I'll move back in.'

'Let us understand each other,' she said in a voice

that was steadier than she felt. 'You wish me to be your housekeeper and child-minder.'

'Whatever you want to call it,' he said impatiently. 'Does it matter?'

'Yes, it matters. It will be impossible unless we define our precise relationship.'

'Very well. Housekeeper and child-minder.'

'And you will give me a proper contract of employment, defining my precise duties, and my salary?'

'Very well.'

'All right,' she said very quietly. 'I'll do it.'

It would be hard. He saw her as a convenience. But at least now she need not leave him for a while. Her heart would break in the end. But not just yet.

Myra returned with coffee, which neither of the others wanted.

'Got it all sorted?' she sang out. 'Jolly good. By the way, Andrew, Simon thinks you invited him. Don't let him guess otherwise.'

'Don't worry, he won't,' Elinor said. 'I'll see to that.' She was beginning to reappraise Myra.

Myra beamed at her. 'I knew you wouldn't let me down.' She flicked open her cell phone. 'Joe? You can come for me in fifteen minutes.' She hung up. 'I'll go and say goodbye to Simon.'

She tripped away, apparently oblivious to the tension between the other two.

'Thank you,' he said. 'I can't think straight. She just sprung this on me—'

'Well, maybe she needed to,' Elinor observed lightly.

'You're on her side?'

'I'm on your little boy's side. I think he's getting

a raw deal. He's much too quiet and docile for his age. When is he ever naughty?'

'I don't know.'

'I'll bet he never is. And he ought to be. Come on, let's go.' She headed for the door.

'Where are we going?'

'Upstairs, so that he can see you and Myra together, and know that you're in complete accord about his being here. I think you should stand together, and if possible put your arm around her shoulders. And smile at her.'

'That's a lot to ask.'

'It's not really, but even if it is, he's your son. Isn't he worth the effort?'

'Of course, but—'

'Then do it,' she said in a voice that brooked no argument.

She didn't know what had made her take a high hand with him, unless it was the memory of Simon's face, beaming at the sight of his father, but cautiously holding back.

He followed her unwillingly upstairs and along to the room that had been Simon's and was now Hetta's.

'We're staying here after all,' she told her daughter. 'You don't mind coming in with me, do you? Then Simon can have his room back.'

'It's all right,' the little boy said at once. 'Hetta can have it, honest.'

'No, it's yours,' Hetta responded.

'You can have it.'

'No, *you* can.'

'No, *you* can.'

'We'll fight about it later,' Elinor said.

She gave Andrew a determined look and he came

forward. 'How about staying here with me, son?' he said. 'Your mother and I thought it would be a good idea.'

'Can I really, Daddy?'

The child's eager face brought home to Andrew that Elinor had been right. It meant the world to Simon to think that his father wanted him. He put his arm awkwardly around Myra's shoulder. 'You don't mind letting me have him for a while, do you?'

'Not if that's what you want,' she responded.

'It's what I want.'

'Is it what Simon wants?' Elinor asked.

The little boy nodded so vigorously that it seemed as though his head might come off. Suddenly his world was full of sunshine, and his father regarded him with shock.

There was a ring on the doorbell below.

'Time for me to go,' Myra said. She gave Simon a hug, then Hetta. Then she turned her expectant gaze on Andrew, who dutifully pecked her cheek. Finally she enveloped Elinor in a scented embrace.

'Thank you,' she whispered in her ear. 'Good luck.'

'Trust me,' Elinor murmured back.

Then she was gone, whisked away by her chauffeur in her glossy car.

'Hetta, you and I will move your things while Simon catches up with his dad,' Elinor said. 'Why don't you two go downstairs, and talk in peace?'

Andrew took orders from nobody except Elmer Rylance, and these days even Rylance usually deferred to him. But he sensed that Elinor knew what she was doing, and right now that made him grateful, so he followed his son downstairs and prepared to embark on a conversation where he knew he would be awkward and probably make mistakes.

Simon soon made it easier for him, smiling happily at having his father's attention, and chattering of what he'd been doing in the last few weeks. Andrew watched him with a kind of aching delight that this sharp-witted, attractive child was his. Somewhere there must be a way to tell him so. But for all the precise, scientific, brilliant words that hummed in his brain, somehow he couldn't locate the right ones for this.

But tonight a kind fate was with him. Simon was in a mood to interpret even his father's silences as interest, and somehow they got through an hour without mishap. But he was relieved when Elinor came down to fetch the child to bed.

When she came down alone, twenty minutes later, she found him pacing restlessly.

'You seemed to manage fairly well there,' she said.

'Mostly due to Simon. I don't understand, he was so different to the way he normally is with me,' he said.

'Because Myra told him you invited him.'

'She said that for her own reasons,' Andrew said scornfully.

'What does it matter what her reasons were? She said what he needed to hear, and it made him happy. All you have to do is catch the ball and run with it.'

'If I'm taking advice I'd rather it was yours,' he said curtly. 'You seem more of a success as a mother.'

'All right, think of Samson. You told me that night that you let your child patients believe their toys had stayed with them because that was what they needed

to think. "It's a deception, but it makes them happy."
That's what you said. Why can't you do the same for
Simon?'

He stared. 'Are you suggesting that I'm only pretending to love him? Because if so, you couldn't be
more wrong.'

'Then tell him. If the love's there, *tell* him.'

'It's easy for you. You'd know how to say things
like that, but I—' He made a helpless gesture. 'When
I'm dealing with him I'm all at sea.'

'But why? He's a lovely child, and he adores you.
Why can't you just relate to him in the way that he
wants?'

'Because I've never known how. At first it was
because I was away so much, but then I didn't know
what to say to him to make it right when I did get
home.'

'Couldn't Myra have helped you?'

'By the time we realised what was wrong, Myra
and I were too far apart to help each other with anything.'

'Well, she helped you this time. Andrew, you don't
have very much time left to get this right. Soon he'll
look elsewhere for his friends, and have his own life
and interests. If you don't catch him now, it'll be too
late.'

'*I know that.* But it doesn't mean I can do anything
about it.' He looked at her. 'But you're here now, and
it'll be all right. You won't try to leave again, will
you?'

She was about to make the biggest mistake of her
life. She should run now, while she still had a last
chance.

'No, I won't leave,' she said. 'I'll stay as long as
you need me.'

CHAPTER ELEVEN

Life assumed a strange, peaceful rhythm of its own. Andrew moved his things back into the house the next day, but for a while they saw little of him. His hours at the hospital were long and he was repeatedly called away for emergencies. He breakfasted with them when he could, and those meals were easier than Elinor had feared. The kids backchatted each other in a way that relieved tension and if Andrew didn't actually join in at least he listened without impatience.

Oddly there was less tension between herself and him than she had feared, which she attributed to the fact that she'd insisted on proper employment conditions and a contract. It was there in black and white. She was Mrs Elinor Landers, housekeeper and childminder. The dreadful night he'd awoken in her arms had happened to somebody else.

Daisy had reacted strangely when Elinor had called her to tell her about the change of plan. 'That's right, love,' she said cheerfully. 'You stay there with him. You never know.'

'I'm his housekeeper,' she said firmly. 'And you couldn't be more wrong.'

'If you say so, love.'

The first time Andrew managed a reasonably early night Simon was waiting for him.

'Ellie said you might be early,' he said excitedly.

'Nine o'clock isn't early, you should be in bed, and who said you could call her Ellie?'

Simon became nervous at his father's frown. 'I thought—she said it was her name.'

He dropped to one knee so that he could look his son in the eye.

'She said that? She actually told you that her name was Ellie?'

'Yes. Isn't it?'

'Yes, it is.'

'Then—I don't understand.'

'There's a lot I don't understand myself, son. Never mind. And don't tell her about this conversation.'

As Elinor had guessed Simon was the perfect companion for Hetta. Her nature was boisterous and now that her strength was returning she could give it fuller rein. By contrast he was shy and retiring, and when they got up to mischief it was Hetta who made the running, with Simon making vain efforts to restrain her, and Fudge bringing up the rear.

Hetta had slept in her mother's room for only a couple of nights. Then Elinor had opened up the room next door to Simon's, and made it hers. But her favourite occupation was to sit with Simon at his computer. At seven he was already literate and an expert at information technology. Hetta, whose education had suffered because of her illness, was fascinated by the things he knew, and her admiration drew him out. Several times Elinor would discover a light beneath Simon's door in the late evening. Entering, she would find the two of them deep in earnest conversation, which would stop as soon as they saw her. She would simply point and Hetta would scuttle away.

'There are things we need to discuss,' she told Andrew one evening when the children were in bed.

'You're not happy with the arrangement?'

'No, it's fine, but school will be starting soon, and I'll need to organise something.'

'When Simon lived here before, he went to the school in the village. It's excellent. I suggest you enrol them both.'

'Good. One more thing.' She took a deep breath. 'When can you take some time off?'

'Goodness knows—'

'It should be in the next three weeks, before school starts, so that Simon can have you all to himself for several days.' He looked at her, and she grew annoyed. 'Surely an organised man like you can arrange suitable cover in that time? You carried Sir Elmer's load while he was sick. Tell him it's your turn.'

'This isn't the best moment for that,' he mused.

'You mean because he'll be retiring soon, the sharks are circling and your teeth are sharper than anyone's. Fine. I'll tell Simon that his father's a shark.'

'Aren't you being a little unfair?'

'No.'

He became angry. 'I really want that job. You're acting as though I'm being unreasonable.'

'You *are* being unreasonable. There are a hundred jobs. You've only got one son.'

'And what are we going to say to each other "for several days"?'

'It doesn't matter. Talk about the weather, anything. The point is that he'll know you put yourself out to be with him. That'll cover a multitude of sins, and Hetta and I will fill in the gaps.'

'Oh, you'll be there?'

She looked at him with pity. 'I wasn't planning to

despatch the two of you to a desert island. Although it might do you some good.'

'Fine. You'll be here. But people still need to talk. It's hard for me to know what to say to him.'

'Who's asking you to say anything? Maybe he'd rather you listened. I expect when you're at work people listen to you, don't they?'

'Usually,' he admitted. 'Unless it's patients, and then I listen.'

'I don't think that covers this situation. You're not in the listening habit, but if you listened to what Simon wants you to hear you might be able to think of some answers. It's not rocket science.'

'No, it's more complicated than that. But you can do it, can't you?' He frowned. 'How?'

She was amused. 'Andrew, you can't take lessons in it. If you could, you'd be marvellous.'

'Yes, I'm good at anything I can study,' he said wryly. 'And maybe you can take lessons with a first rate teacher. That's why I watch you so closely. You seem to know everything that I don't.'

'Andrew, will you tell me something? Why didn't you just let Simon go to America with Myra?'

'Because he's all I've got to love,' he said simply. 'I've made a mess of every other important relationship. I don't really know how to talk to anyone who means anything to me. Oh, I'm fine with the patients, not just the children, but the adults too. It's easy, because I know what they expect of me, and it's very limited.'

'Limited? Saving their lives?'

'In a way, yes. They come into the hospital and I can be their best friend. I chat with the children, discuss soccer scores and newspaper stories with the adults. Then we pass out of each other's lives without regret. Emotionally they expect nothing from me.'

'You weren't always like that,' she said.

'Yes, I was, potentially. With you I found a way to be different.'

'You mean, this is what I did to you?'

'I wasn't blaming you. You asked me something, and I tried to find a rational explanation.'

'Must everything be rational?'

'It usually is, in the end.'

'Andrew, do you believe that, or is it what you try to tell yourself?'

He sighed. 'Does it matter?'

When he'd gone upstairs she wandered out into the garden with Fudge, who still had matters to attend to. She waited for him, sitting on a bench under the trees.

'May I join you?' It was Andrew with two glasses of wine.

She received one gratefully and he sat down beside her, looking up at the moon, which hung low in the sky, bright and silver. It was a night for lovers, but just now she felt only contentment.

'By the way,' she said after a moment, 'don't forget a wedding present for Myra.'

'Why would I want to do that? She's getting her hands on the Hellerman millions.'

'It's in the cause of good relations. It'll make Simon happy.'

'Then I'll do it. Or rather you'll do it.'

'No, Simon will do it. He's searched the Internet and found a great store in Detroit. All he needs now is your credit card.'

'Fine. I trust you to make sure he doesn't clean me out.'

Through Simon's daily phone calls with Myra they followed the progress of her wedding. Backed by Cyrus's gold card she'd embarked on a spending spree, not always with happy results. A dozen pictures of her in various prospective wedding outfits turned up on Simon's computer. He and Hetta regarded them with awe, which Elinor fully understood when she joined them. Andrew returned one evening to find the three of them gazing at the screen.

'Something interesting?' he asked, walking over. 'Why is your mother in a scarlet satin dress?'

'To get married in?' Simon said, making it a question.

'Really.' Andrew pursed his lips and said no more. To Elinor's pleasure, man and boy regarded each other in silent masculine sympathy.

With Elinor's guidance Simon had chosen some elegant silver for the wedding gift. Myra was genuinely pleased, pretending to believe the fiction that Andrew had thought of it. She even sent him an email saying thank you, which Simon presented to him with pride.

At last the wedding pictures themselves arrived. Myra had avoided red satin and purple velvet in favour of a comparatively restrained dress of ivory brocade. Everything else was over the top, including six bridesmaids and four page-boys who, for no discernible reason, were dressed in highland kilts.

'Are you sorry you weren't there?' Andrew asked his son.

Simon gave him a speaking look. 'Mum would have wanted me to be a page-boy.'

'Then you were definitely better off out of it.'

Every day Elinor set her mind to finding ways to

help Andrew connect with his son. She joined in the children's games, she made Simon talk to her, and he did so with a freedom that showed how badly he longed to confide. She remembered how good Andrew had been at chess, and it was no surprise to discover that at seven Simon was already a skilled player.

Once she'd discovered that she went onto the attack, buying a newspaper with a daily chess problem and getting him to solve it. Then she tried to arrange it so that Simon was sitting over the problem when Andrew arrived home. This was hard as Andrew's arrivals could seldom be predicted, but one night she struck lucky. Best of all Simon was so absorbed that he failed to look up when his father entered, something rare enough to make Andrew stride across to see what was engrossing his son, and had to speak to him twice before he could get his attention. After that they worked on the problem together, and Elinor chalked up a minor victory.

'I didn't even know he could play,' he told Elinor that evening as she was making a late-night snack.

'He's pretty good.'

'Yes, he is.'

'As good as you at that age?'

'I think so.' He looked at her shrewdly. 'Was it an accident, what happened tonight?'

'Of course not. I got him into position a few minutes before you got home. But you did the rest yourself.'

'When I employed you as child-minder I didn't envisage you going this far.'

'I'm like you. I like to do my job properly. Besides,

the way I see it, I still owe you for Hetta's life. If I can help you with Simon, we're quits.'

'I see,' he said quietly. 'Yes, I never thought of it like that.'

After that there were some phone calls that she didn't understand, or, rather, didn't ask about. She found herself talking to a woman with a voice like cut glass, who turned out to be the secretary of Sir Elmer Rylance. She fetched Andrew to the phone and returned to the children, trying not to speculate.

She made no further mention of his taking time off, and nor did he. She concluded that he'd either forgotten the matter or dismissed it. She was angry with him. She didn't press the matter, but she had a sense of failure. She'd tried to believe that in this matter at least she could be good for him, but it seemed that he now dismissed her opinions as easily as he did everyone else's.

Only when she'd totally given up hope did he arrive home one evening and say, 'That's it! No more hospital for a week.'

The children bounded about in excitement. Over their heads Andrew met her eyes with a look that startled her. It was almost as though he was asking for her approval.

'Why did you keep it to yourself until now?' she asked when she could make herself heard through the riot.

'I wasn't sure until the last minute. It depended on whether my replacement arrived in time, but he did.'

'Is he as good as you?' she couldn't resist asking.

He looked at her. 'Almost. He thinks he's better.'

'If he's so brilliant, how come he's available?'

'He's been offered three other jobs, but the one he

wants is Elmer's, so he's been keeping himself free. He jumped at this.'

Of course he would, Elinor thought. It was the chance to work under Rylance's nose and pip the other candidates to the post. And Andrew had stood back and let him do it, because she'd as good as asked him to. But her stab of pleasure was quickly suppressed. He'd done it for Simon, not her. And it might be a disaster for him.

Too late now to say anything. It was done. And Andrew was already going into the garden with the children.

He joined her later that night for their regular glass of wine while Fudge snuffled in the undergrowth.

'Could your replacement really harm you?' she asked.

'In one week?' he demanded. 'You don't think much of my skill.'

'A determined man can do a lot in a week.'

'He can do his worst,' Andrew said arrogantly. 'I gather you think I might soon be on my uppers. That's a pity, because I was going to suggest that we should get married.'

'*What?*' She tried to see him but there was no moon tonight and she could only make out his shape. His face was hidden from her.

'It makes a lot of sense, Ellie. We make a pretty good family. Simon loves you and he's crazy about Hetta.'

'Just a minute—'

'We have to think where this arrangement is going. If we don't marry then sooner or later we'll split up. You're an excellent employee, but employees leave. I want you to stay.'

'It takes a lot more than that to make a family,' she said in a toneless voice. She'd thought Andrew had hurt her in every possible way, but she hadn't thought of this. Marry her to keep a good employee!

'Of course it does, but I'm sure we can make it work. I'm probably not putting this very well, but if you'll only give it some thought—for everyone's sake—'

'Everyone? Does that include me?'

He stared at her, trying to discern on her face what had disturbed him in her voice. 'You don't think this might be a good idea for you?'

'I don't think there could be a worse idea for me. I've told you I'll stay while you need me, but I'm making a condition. Don't ever, ever mention this again.'

She rose and walked away towards the house, with Fudge trotting after her, leaving him sitting alone in the darkness.

It was Andrew who noticed that there was a funfair about a mile away, and he who suggested that they should go. He was also the one to set the date.

'The day after tomorrow,' he said, 'because that's Ellie's birthday.'

Hetta stared. 'How did you know? I didn't tell you.'

'I'm a magician,' he said, and that satisfied her.

'I don't want to make a fuss about my birthday,' she muttered as soon as they were alone.

'Too late. Give your friend Daisy a call and ask her to stay with us that night.'

It would be good to see Daisy again, but she would inevitably take over the children, leaving her too much with Andrew. She'd been steering clear of him ever since he'd made her that insulting offer of marriage, but it was hard now he was at home for the week. He strode off without waiting for an answer, and a few minutes later he departed on a gift-buying expedition with the children.

When her birthday came they all made the breakfast, then plied her with gifts. From Hetta there was a brooch in the shape of a heart, and from Simon a pair of slippers. Andrew's gift was a scarf, made of wool and silk. It was exquisite and expensive, but not so much as to invite comment. She thanked him quietly, and promised to wear it that evening.

The taxi arrived with Daisy, and now she was glad her old friend was there to shield her from the attention. Her thoughts had been in turmoil ever since the other night. There had been a brief temptation to say yes, marry him anyway and count on her own love to be enough.

Try as she might, she couldn't stop her thoughts wandering down that path. To the outside world they looked like a family, two parents and two children. It was tempting to think that they really were a family, to pretend that she were his wife, as she might once have been.

These days, when he took the children into the village, and the three of them returned to find her getting them a snack in the kitchen, they would greet each other with smiles, and for a moment she could think, *This is how it would be if we were married.*

And it could still happen. She could tell him she'd reconsidered and decided that it was a sensible idea. But the word 'sensible' checked her. Her love alone would never be enough for the two of them, and only misery could come from trying to make it.

On the afternoon of her birthday the phone rang. Elinor was alone when she answered it, and she was immediately glad.

'Hi, sweetie,' came Myra's voice singing down the line. 'How's tricks?'

'We're doing very well,' Elinor said. 'Do you want to talk to Simon?'

'Thanks, but I just got off the line to him an hour ago.'

'How's Detroit?'

'Hot. Muggy. But Cyrus is letting me have the swimming pool enlarged. I thought of making it like a Roman bath house. What do you think?'

'I think it'll be very "you",' Elinor said.

Myra's crack of laughter showed that she fully understood this tact. 'I called to say happy birthday!' she said.

'Thank you. How did you know?'

'Simon told me. He says you're going out on this great party. Big funfair.'

'That's right. An old friend of mine is here, so there'll be three of us looking out for the children.'

'Good, have a great time. And listen, I have a birthday gift for you.'

'That's very kind. I'll look forward to it.'

'No, I'm going to give it to you now. I knew I'd seen you somewhere before as soon as we met, and now it's come to me. It's you in that photograph.'

'What photograph?'

'The one Andrew keeps with him. Or I should say *one* of the ones he keeps with him. There's about a dozen of them. Him and this girl with masses of blonde hair, sitting together, their arms around each other, kissing. And sometimes just her on her own. He didn't know that I knew. I found them in his desk drawer one day, and I never told him. So you were the ghost.'

'The ghost?'

'Andrew's ghost, the one that's always haunted him. I knew soon after we married that there was someone else. I don't mean another woman in the conventional sense, but a secret ghost in his heart that he visited sometimes, and came back looking sad. I was arrogant enough to think I could drive her away, but I never could, because she was the one he loved.'

'Myra, I'm sure you're wrong about this—'

'No, I'm not wrong. It's your face.'

'Yes, it's me, but the rest—we were children. At least, I was.'

'But he wasn't,' Myra said shrewdly. 'One thing I know about Andrew, he gives all of himself to everything. It's exhausting to live with, but the one who really gets dragged through the mill is Andrew.'

'Yes,' Elinor murmured. 'It was like that. I did love him but I was seventeen and all of him was more than I could cope with. If we'd met later—' She sighed.

'Has he been a ghost for you too, then?'

'All the time,' she said slowly, realising that it was true. 'I never meant to keep thinking of him, but somehow he wouldn't go away. I could never forget how badly I'd treated him and it spoiled everything else. And his face on the last day—yes, I suppose that's been my ghost.'

'And you're not going to look me in the eyes and

say you don't still love him, are you?' Myra demanded, blithely ignoring the miles separating them.

'Myra—'

'Of course you're not. It stands out a mile. There was always a third person in our marriage,' she added, without rancour. 'It's fascinating to meet her after all this time.'

'I'm sorry.'

'Don't be. It wasn't your fault. Andrew and I should never have married. Once you'd had the "all" there wasn't much left for anyone else. What happens next is up to you, but for Andrew's sake I hope you get your act together. Bye, sweetie. Have a nice birthday.' She hung up.

Elinor set down the phone, her mind whirling. It couldn't be true. Myra had somehow got it wrong. And yet there was something in the word 'ghost' that had caught at her heart. She'd been haunted since the day of their parting, and of course Andrew had been haunted too.

But he'd been cured when they'd met again and he'd seen how she'd changed. She must remember that.

Both children were persuaded to sleep the afternoon away, under the dire threat of having to leave the funfair early. They set out in the early evening, with both youngsters bright-eyed and eager.

Andrew was an unexpected success. The same skills that made him a surgeon made him score bull's-eyes at the coconut shy, which he did so often that the harassed owner ordered him off, to the children's hilarity.

'Oh, look, Mummy, there's a big wheel.' Hetta tugged on Elinor's hand. 'Can we go on it?'

'It looks awfully big, darling,' Elinor said, looking up doubtfully.

'That's the idea,' Andrew observed, following her gaze. 'You're not scared, are you, Ellie?'

'You know I am,' she said softly.

She wondered what was happening. There was something different about Andrew tonight, as though he was determined to provoke her memories.

'Come along,' Daisy carolled, leading the way to the entrance. Simon and Hetta went with her, and the three of them piled in together.

'Come along,' Andrew said, taking Elinor's hand, and soon they were in the seat just behind the others.

Then they were off, sailing silently upward, higher and higher, until they reached the top and began the stomach-churning descent. But her nerves seemed unimportant because Andrew's arm was about her shoulders, drawing her close.

'Andrew, we agreed—I'm just an employee.'

'No, you agreed that. Tonight you're Ellie. You've always been Ellie. You always will be. Do you remember?' he whispered as his lips brushed on hers.

'Yes, everything.'

'Do you remember what I said to you that night?'

'You said you'd been plotting for ages how to kiss me.'

'"And I'm such a coward that I waited until now, when you can't escape,"' he quoted. 'I'm no braver now. I had to do it again. Kiss me, Ellie. Kiss me for ever.'

She couldn't resist any longer. She threw her arms about him, kissing him fiercely as she had done that first time, while the wheel spun and the stars rained down on them.

CHAPTER TWELVE

EVERYONE agreed that it had been the best night out ever. At home they toasted the occasion in hot chocolate before Daisy and Elinor chivvied the children upstairs.

'Then I'm going straight to bed myself,' Daisy said.

'Me too,' Elinor agreed. 'Goodnight, Andrew.'

The jollity continued as they climbed the stairs and put their giggling charges to bed. They didn't want the day to end, but at last they dropped off to sleep. Elinor kissed Daisy goodnight and went to her own room.

She undressed mechanically, trying to sort out her turbulent thoughts, but knowing it was impossible. Something had happened tonight that had brought about a change in Andrew. It had been happening gradually, she realised, but tonight was different. On top of the wheel he'd spoken of having no courage, but he'd acted like a man who'd finally decided to take his courage in his hands.

When the soft knock came on her door she knew she'd been listening for it for a long time.

Andrew stood there looking hesitant until she stood back for him to pass. He was still dressed in the trousers and shirt he'd worn all evening, the shirt open at the throat. He had something in his hand.

'There's something you ought to see,' he said, offering it to her.

It was an envelope, containing the very photographs Myra had described to her over the phone. Elinor went through them slowly. There were the two of them in each other's arms, oblivious to whoever had been holding the camera, oblivious to all the world but each other.

'We were so young,' she murmured. 'I always knew that I was, but you too—I never realised. Why do you bring me these now?'

'Because I understand you already know about them.'

She stared at him. 'Myra?'

'She called me and said she'd spoken to you earlier.'

'Did she tell you what she'd said to me?'

'The gist of it. Enough to make it clear that I couldn't put this off any longer. There's so much I want to say to you, and I've delayed saying it in case it drove you away.'

'Is it about the past?'

'Yes.'

'Do you think we should risk it? Is there any more to say?'

'There's this to say. Ellie—do you think you can ever forgive me?'

'Shouldn't it be me asking you for forgiveness?'

'No. Everything that happened was my fault. You were so young. You wanted to enjoy yourself and explore life, as you had every right to. And I tried to tie you down long before you were ready.

'Everything you said about me that day was right. I tried to order your life to suit myself. My only excuse is that I knew how badly I needed you. You were my lifeline to the rest of the world. I'd put work and study before everything, and I'd ignored a whole side of myself to do it. Then you brought that part of me back to life, and I knew I had to keep you with me, at all costs. But what I never saw, or wouldn't let myself see, was that the cost was paid by you.

'I drove you into Jack Smith's arms. But for me you'd never have looked at him. Which means that all the bad things that have happened to you since then have been my fault.'

'No, that's too hard. What about what I did to you?'

'Nothing I didn't deserve. If I'd been more patient, instead of grabbing at you, we might have stayed together, and been together now.'

'Andrew, that time I went to the island with Jack, nothing happened. He tried, but he got his face slapped. I wouldn't have done that to you.'

'Thank you. It's odd, after all these years, how much it still means to hear you say that.'

'I wanted you to be the first, and you should have been.'

'Yes, if I hadn't been so smugly determined that my way was right, we could just have found a flat together until you were ready to commit yourself.'

'Lived as brother and sister, you mean?' she asked, gently teasing.

'Blow that! I could barely keep my hands off you, and you made it as hard as you could.'

She stood still a moment, thinking of that time and the life they might have had. 'If only...' she said longingly.

'There are a million if onlys,' he said, stroking her hair.

'If only we'd met a few years later. Just think—'

'I do think,' he said harshly. 'And then I try not to think of it, because it's the way to go mad. For a while after it happened I believe I actually did go crazy. I turned myself into an automaton. I shut off every softer feeling because I had no use for them any more. When I allowed myself to feel emotions again I made sure they were kept in neat order.

'But then I saw you that day in the hospital corridor, and my whole orderly world went haywire. When we talked and I heard how you'd been forced to live I knew what I'd done to you. I was beside myself, but at least I had the chance to help you. I thought I'd do the operation, Hetta would recover, we'd go our separate ways and I'd feel better about you.

'But then you were homeless, and the temptation was too much for me. I told you a fairy tale to get you here, and I trapped myself because I didn't dare visit you. I was afraid if you knew the truth you'd run away. But I longed to come here. I wanted to see you in my home, as you always should have been. I used to think of you, living here, and pretend that you were my wife. Foolish, eh?'

'Not so foolish as you think,' she murmured, remembering her own pretence.

'What was that?'

'Nothing,' she said hurriedly. 'Go on.' She was holding her breath for whatever came next.

'Then you called me, and I came over that night, and it all went wrong. You were so upset about the money, and when you came to my bed—you don't know how much I wanted you. But not like that. Not because you felt you owed me.'

She stared. 'Is that what you thought? That it was a kind of payment?'

'What else could I think? You so hated taking anything from me, especially money. And then there you
were in bed with me, and I thought I heard you saying
all the sweet things I wanted to hear from you. I
didn't know whether you were really saying them, or
whether it was just a dream. I'd had that kind of
dream so often. Then I awoke and you were making
love to me, and I thought you were doing it as some
kind of duty. It was a nightmare.'

'But it wasn't that at all,' she breathed. 'You were
wretched and I wanted to be close to you, and love
you. When you pushed me away I thought I'd embarrassed you because you didn't want me.'

'Didn't want you?' he echoed. 'There hasn't been
a moment in the last twelve years when I haven't
loved you and wanted you, even when I wouldn't
admit it to myself. But after that night I felt I'd driven
you off. You started planning to leave, but then Myra
turned up with Simon, and suddenly I had a second
chance. If you knew how my heart sank when you
started talking about being my housekeeper and child-
minder, and contracts of employment.'

'I was trying to tell you I wouldn't throw myself
at you. I thought it would relieve your mind.'

'But I asked you to marry me.'

'To hold onto a good employee. That's what you
said.'

'Yes, that's what I *said*. I thought you didn't care
about me. I played it cool just to get that ring on your
finger. After we were married I could tell you I'd
loved you all the time, and always would. Well, anyway, you didn't fall for it, so I changed tack. There
had to be some way to woo you. Then I remembered
it was your birthday, the anniversary of the day we'd

met, and there was the funfair and maybe I could—'
He broke off and sighed. 'I haven't improved, have
I? I'm still thinking about what I want, trying to grab
you, and never mind whether you love me or not.'

'You thought I didn't love you?'

'I was sure of it—until today, when Myra told me
some of the things you'd said to her. And then I began
to hope.'

'Hope? I loved you with all my heart. I wouldn't
marry you because you just wanted a secure employee.'

Andrew looked at her, his heart in his eyes. 'Oh,
Ellie,' he said. 'How we misunderstand each other.
We always have. Shall we ever get it right? Or shall
we keep getting it wrong and love each other anyway?'

His words had a curious effect on her. It was what
she'd longed for, but suddenly all she could see was
that the past had made the future confused, perhaps
impossible.

'Andrew—'

'What is it, my darling?'

She backed away from him. 'Don't say things like
that.'

'But why? Unless I've fooled myself and you can't
love me again.'

'I still love you,' she burst out, 'but maybe it's too
late. How can we get it back—what we had? The
people we were then don't exist any more.'

'Ellie—Ellie—'

'Don't call me that,' she cried. 'She's dead, gone.
I can't be Ellie any more.'

He took hold of her. 'Look at me,' he said, raising
her face and brushing back her hair. 'Let me see your

face. It's the face I've always loved. It hasn't changed with the years except to become sadder and gentler. It's still beautiful, still Ellie, still my love.'

He kissed her before she could reply. Then kissed her again. She stopped trying to struggle and relaxed in his arms, knowing she had no power to fight something she wanted with all her heart. The problems were still waiting for them, but first she would enjoy her love.

'Ellie…'

'Yes, my love, yes—'

'Do you still want me?'

'Always.'

He slipped off her robe. Underneath was one of her matronly nightgowns, which she wore almost as a uniform these days, but his fingers got to work, undoing the buttons and pushing it so that it fell to the floor, and there was the body he loved.

'Did you think you could hide from me like this?' he murmured, his lips against her skin. 'You could dress like an Eskimo and I'd still pick you out from a million as the most beautiful woman in the world.'

Twice before she'd offered herself to him, but only now could he accept the gift. She sensed his eagerness as she undressed him in turn. When they were both naked he drew her down onto the bed for the loving that had waited too long.

After all these years they approached this moment as strangers, hopeful but unsure. He was broader, less wiry, more powerful than she recalled, but with a gentleness that was unchanged. Time and sadness had added a new dimension to her, and he searched her face as he made love to her, seeking to fathom her secrets, knowing that in the end it couldn't be done.

She had told him that he should have been the first, but in one sense he was. After two husbands he was still her first true lover, the first man to take her into another world and show her wonders. It was awesome, almost alarming, but when she looked into his face she knew she could never be afraid as long as he was with her.

She saw something else too—that in her arms he'd found the fulfilment no other woman could ever have brought him. When their closest union was over, and they lay side by side, it wasn't the end of love-making, merely a different stage. She had never known that such peace was possible. In the moments after desire was fulfilled and the fire faded, only love and tenderness were left.

'I told you I wouldn't let you go,' he said softly as she lay cradled in his arms. 'And now I never will. Let's get married quickly.'

She stirred. 'Andrew, wait, please. It's a little soon to start talking about marriage. We've only just found each other.'

'That's why it's so important not to lose each other again.'

'I don't want that either—' she tried to sit up but he drew her firmly down beside him '—but we could lose each other again if we're not careful. No, listen to me—' She fended him off as he tried to kiss her. 'After twelve years we're different people, and we don't really know who those other people are. We both have years of secrets.'

'There'll never be any secrets between us from now on, I promise. If we know that we love each other the rest can come. Darling—'

He stopped, seeing the sudden unease in her eyes, and his hands fell from her.

'Oh, no!' he said, in a horrified voice. 'I'm doing it again, aren't I? Trying to hurry you into doing what I want.' He got up with a convulsive movement. 'And if you listen to me it'll end the same way.'

'Darling.' She slid quickly across the bed to where he was sitting on the edge. It hurt her to see him troubled. This was important to her, but she moved swiftly to comfort him, putting her arms about him and resting her head against his back. 'Don't make so much of it. I just want a little time to know you, and not make the same mistakes as last time. I love you. I always will.'

'Then why—?' He checked himself quickly. 'Never mind, we'll do it your way.' He turned back to her, revealing himself at an angle that aroused her immediate interest.

'Whatever I want?' she asked, craning her head to see better. 'Anything at all?'

He stroked her head tenderly. 'Your wish is my command.'

'In that case, come here.' She pulled him towards her.

Andrew tensed suddenly.

'What is it?' she asked.

'I thought I heard a noise.'

They listened together, but there was only silence in the darkened house.

'Come back,' she said, drawing him close again.

But the next moment they both heard the noise, footsteps coming up the stairs and the sound of a voice that they both recognised.

'Thanks a bunch, Daisy. Don't worry, I know my way.'

'I don't believe it,' Andrew said, appalled. 'It can't be.'

'I've got a terrible feeling that it is,' Elinor breathed.

The next moment the door opened. Andrew had just enough time to pull the sheet over him before Myra swept into the room.

'Surprise!' she cried.

'Myra, how did you get here?' Elinor asked, aghast. 'You were in Detroit this afternoon!'

'I didn't actually say I was.'

'No, you never did,' she realised.

'I arrived yesterday to stay with Uncle Elmer. He wanted me here for his big weekend.'

'Never mind that,' Andrew said hastily.

'Which means you haven't told Ellie.'

Elinor looked at Andrew. 'Secrets?' she asked quietly.

'I'll explain later,' he growled. 'Not with her here.'

'I got suspicious when you weren't at Uncle Elmer's weekend,' Myra said.

'Maybe I was trying to avoid you,' Andrew suggested.

'Oh, no, darling. Uncle Elmer's house party is a step up the ladder, and you've never missed one of those. You wouldn't risk damaging your career just to avoid me.'

'Why should a house party affect his career?' Elinor asked.

'Because Uncle Elmer is about to nominate his successor, and he has rather old fashioned ideas about surgeons. He doesn't think medical skill is enough.

To him a heart surgeon should be a great man who rides loftily above the rest of society.'

'Rubbish,' Andrew snapped.

'But you should have been there,' Elinor cried.

'Tonight was the big banquet,' Myra said.

'Tonight I had something better to do,' Andrew said.

'Go to a funfair, I believe. And for that, you snubbed his big weekend, full of the medical glitterati. And I asked myself why you'd do that. Not just because you don't believe in his ideas. In the past you've always done whatever came next, so why not now?' Her eyes flickered over Elinor. 'And I thought I knew the answer. So I came over to see if I was right.'

'And now you know you are, I suppose you're going to make hay with it,' Andrew growled. 'Well, do your worst.'

'No,' Elinor protested, 'Andrew, I know what it means to you—'

'It means nothing to me beside you,' he said. 'Let her tell him anything she likes.'

'And I've got a fair bit to tell him, haven't I?' Myra mused. 'Some people might call this little set-up an unprofessional relationship. Ellie isn't your patient but her daughter is. And moving them into your house, bringing Ellie into your bed—I think the General Medical Council would have a field day.'

'Myra, you wouldn't,' Elinor cried in horror. Surely she couldn't have been wrong about Myra, who had seemed good-natured despite her touch of hardness?

'I might,' Myra said. 'I might do anything, unless, of course, you draw my claws before I do it.'

'I see,' Andrew said in disgust. 'Blackmail.'

'Hmm. A kind of.'

'So what do you want?'

'Well, if you two were to tell the world that you were going to get married it would all become quite respectable, wouldn't it? It wouldn't matter what I said. Even Uncle Elmer would approve.'

'But—' Andrew hesitated, then said with difficulty, 'about getting married—there's a problem—'

'Oh, don't be stupid, darling, of course there isn't. Don't tell me the two of you are going to make the same mistake again. Andrew, when we talked this afternoon I gave you the key to Ellie, but something told me you were going fumble it. Why, I can't imagine. She's not going to run out on you this time. She's as nuts about you as you are about her.'

'Myra,' Elinor protested, almost laughing as she realised that Myra was, after all, a good, if unorthodox, friend, 'it's not that simple.'

'Yes, it is. Things usually are simple. You see what you want and go for it. Open your eyes, Ellie. Think what'll happen to Andrew if he loses you again? He isn't a man who loves easily, or often. It was his misfortune, and yours, that he met the ''one and only'' when she was too young. The time was all wrong. Now it's right.'

'It's just that we thought we'd spend a little time getting to know each other first,' Elinor tried to explain. 'We're older now, and we want to go carefully.'

'Whatever for?' Myra demanded, aghast. 'Honestly, sweetie, that's not the way. Just cut the cackle and get on with it. And make it as soon as possible. Next month would be nice. Cyrus and I are coming over here for a publicity do, and I wouldn't miss your wedding for anything.'

Elinor clutched her head. 'This conversation is making me dizzy. How can you be saying these things to me? You were his wife.'

'But I'm not his wife any more. Or if I am, poor Cyrus is deluding himself. I'm sure I married him. Yes, of course I did, I sent you the pictures. By the way, I've got some wedding cake for you all downstairs. All right, all right,' she said quickly, seeing the fulminating look in Andrew's eye. 'I'm very happy, and I'd like to see you both happy too, which, of course, would be the best thing for Simon.'

'And the best for you,' Andrew observed cynically. 'Cyrus really doesn't want your son by your first marriage spending too much time with you, does he?'

'That depends where he is,' Myra said thoughtfully. 'It's fine at Disneyland because he and Simon are about the same mental age and they can enjoy it together. But at other times Simon would be distinctly in the way. But he loves it here with both of you and Hetta. He's told me so when we've talked on the phone. OK, OK, I'm a selfish cow who doesn't want her son cramping her style. But I do love him, and I'd like to see him settled in the place *he* wants to be.'

They stared at her, thunderstruck. In the silence Myra's cell phone shrilled and she answered, 'It's all right, Uncle Elmer, he's here, but I don't think he can talk now. He's got some important business going down. You can call him tomorrow and give him the good news.'

She hung up. 'All right, I've said my piece. Now it's up to you two. Just get on with it.'

She embraced Elinor. 'I'm going now, but you and I will be seeing each other quite often in the future, since you're going to be stepmother to my son.'

'Am I?'

'Of course you are. We just settled it. Didn't you notice? Is Simon in the same room, by the way? I'd better drop in on him before I go.'

She blew Andrew a kiss, waved and headed for the door.

'Myra,' he said quietly, 'thank you for everything.'

'Just don't forget to invite me to the wedding,' she told him. 'I want to give you away.'

She slipped out and from the corridor they heard her say, 'Simon, darling, there you are! Guess what. Daddy and Ellie are getting married. Isn't that lovely? Hetta, dear, you'll just love being a bridesmaid. Pink satin, I think. You've got the perfect complexion for it.'

Her voice faded.

Silence.

'Well,' Elinor spoke cautiously, 'pink satin isn't so bad. As long as she doesn't bring Hetta to our wedding in scarlet satin.'

He put his arms around her and spoke beseechingly. 'Darling Ellie, you don't have to—'

'Of course I do. We both do. It's all been decided. And Myra was right. We should just cut the cackle and get on with it. What was I fretting about?'

'You're not angry that I kept the weekend a secret? Telling you would have felt like emotional blackmail.'

'No, I'm not angry. I can just hardly believe that you took such a risk.'

'To blazes with Elmer and his glitzy weekend. I

wanted to ride on the big wheel with the girl of my dreams. Just like last time. Some things are still the same, Ellie.'

'But think what it might have cost you?'

He held up his hands before her. 'I'll stand or fall by what these can do, not my ability to wear a dinner jacket.'

'Did I hear right? Did Myra say something about good news? I think you got it anyway.'

'Really? I wasn't listening. This is more important. My dearest love, once I tried to pressure you into marriage. I didn't even ask you properly the first time, but I'm asking now. Ellie, will you marry me?'

She took his face gently between her hands.

'Yes, my dearest. I will.'

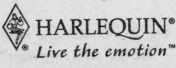

The world's bestselling romance series.

HARLEQUIN®
Presents

Seduction and Passion Guaranteed!

THE PRINCESS BRIDES

For duty, for money...for passion!

Discover a thrilling new trilogy from a rising star of Harlequin Presents®, Jane Porter!

Meet the Royals...

Chantal, Nicolette and Joelle are members of the blue-blooded Ducasse family. Step inside their sophisticated and glamorous world and watch as these beautiful princesses find they have to marry three international playboys—for duty, for money... and definitely for passion!

Don't miss

THE SULTAN'S BOUGHT BRIDE (#2418)
September 2004

THE GREEK'S ROYAL MISTRESS (#2424)
October 2004

THE ITALIAN'S VIRGIN PRINCESS (#2430)
November 2004

Pick up a Harlequin Presents® novel and you will enter a world of spine-tingling passion and provocative, tantalizing romance!

Available wherever Harlequin books are sold.

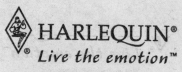

HARLEQUIN®
Live the emotion™

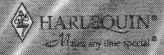

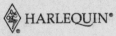